THE SMURFS TALES

Peyo

PAPERCUTZ ™
NEW YORK

THE SMURFS TALES #6

© Peyo - 2022- Licensed through Lafig Belgium - www.smurf.com

SMURF™

"Smurf and Order"
BY PEYO
WITH THE COLLABORATION OF
ALAIN JOST AND THIERRY CULLIFORD FOR THE SCRIPT,
JEROEN DE CONINCK FOR THE ARTWORK,
AND NINE CULLIFORD FOR THE COLORS

"Night of the Sorcerers"
BY PEYO
WITH THE COLLABORATION OF
YVAN DELPORTE AND THIERRY CULLIFORD FOR THE SCRIPT,
ALAIN MAURY FOR THE ARTWORK AND
NINE CULLIFORD FOR THE COLORS

"The Smurf from Outer Space"
BY PEYO
AND HIS STUDIO

"The Smurf Gags"
BY PEYO
AND HIS STUDIO

"The Smurf and the Robot X-XIII"
BY PEYO
AND HIS STUDIO

Joe Johnson, *SMURFLATIONS*
Bryan Senka, Justin Birch, Wilson Ramos Jr., *LETTERING SMURFS*
Léa Zimmerman, *SMURFIC PRODUCTION*
Matt. Murray, *SMURF CONSULTANT*
Stephanie Brooks, *ASSISTANT MANAGING SMURF*
Jim Salicrup, *SMURF-IN-CHIEF*

HC ISBN 978-1-5458-0978-5
PB ISBN 978-1-5458-0976-1

PRINTED IN CHINA
NOVEMBER 2022

Papercutz books may be purchased for business or
promotional use. For information on bulk purchases
please contact Macmillan Corporate and Premium
Sales Department at (800) 221-7945 x5442.

DISTRIBUTED BY MACMILLAN
FIRST PAPERCUTZ PRINTING

SMURF AND ORDER

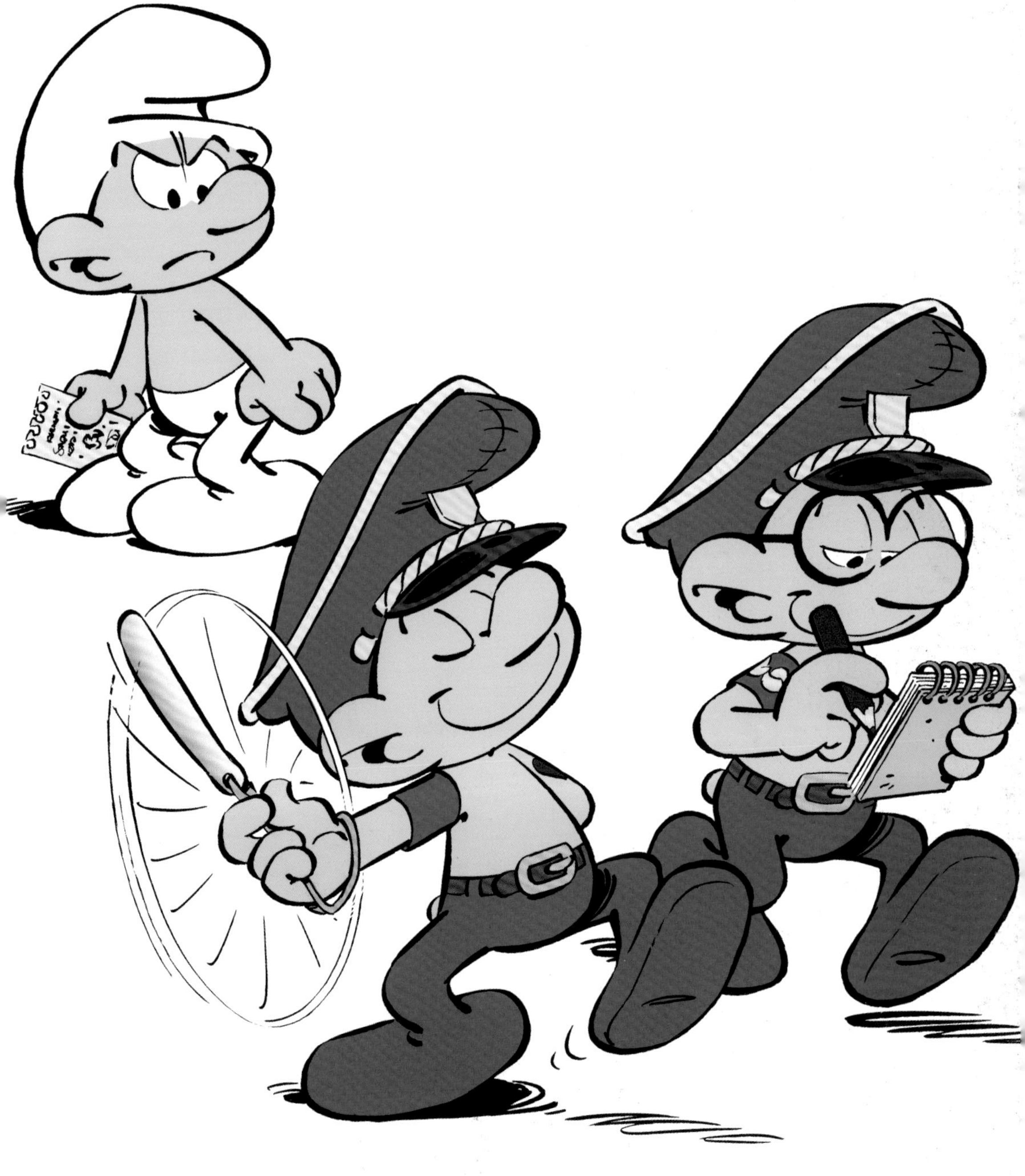

The village of the Smurfs, on this lovely summer afternoon, seems to be the most peaceful place in the world.

ZZZ

SQUEAK
SQUEAK
SQUEAK

You could put some oil on your wheel!

SQUEAK
SQUEAK

Oh! Sorry for dissmurfing your concentration, Lazy Smurf!

This tranquility, however, is fragile. It's hanging by a thread...

Z

Hmm!

I've had it. This can't keep smurfing like this!

*An alchemical substance.

Uh... Are you hurt?

I smurfed a drop of acid on my finger! What got you two smurfing in here like that?

It's because of him. His hedge is so high, it smurfs my plants from growing. And he refuses to trim it!

He's a nosy neighbor. When the hedge is cut, he's always watching what I'm smurfing!

Hmm...

Come now... He wants peace and quiet in his garden, and that's his most important smurf!

HA!

But you could smurf a little goodwill and trim your hedge to the height of a Smurf!

Ah? You hear that?

Um... To the height of a Smurf with a cap?

Of course... Like any respectable Smurf.

Okay, then. I'll go smurf my shears.

That's very smurf of you!

Iaboratory

NO SMURFING

With the little crisis resolved, calm has returned.

Tralala...

Smurflalalalalaaa...

But there are just days like this...

WHAT?

3

For smurf's sake! He's doing it again...

Every time I put my laundry out to dry, you smurf a fire. Put that out right now!

No way -- I started my fire before you smurfed your laundry!

You're nothing but an uncouth smurf!

Let's see what Papa Smurf says about this!

There... The red cinnabar is smurfing onto the neck of the retort! And now...

Papa Smurf? Do you have a minute? We'd like your opinion.

Again?

A minute later...

The next time, you smurf your laundry in the morning. The laundry will be dry already by the afternoon.

And you, when you smurf a fire, do so at sunset. The air is cooler, and the smoke will rise straight up!

Uh... Sure, Papa Smurf!

Now, excuse me... I have a retort over a flame!

He's sure in a bad smurf!

Yes. He's smurfing downright irritable with age!

WHAM

⇨Whew!⇦ Finally, some silence!

4

PWAAAAT

NO WAY! You're not going to be smurfing my ears!

But... The summer fair will happen soon! I have to smurf my exercises!

Go smurf it in the depths of the forest and let me sleep!

Are you kidding me? Nap time is over!

I'm going to go tell Papa Smurf!

Me too!

NOW THAT'S ENOUGH!

I've had enough! You get into arguments over petty smurfs and every time, you come bother me!

If you're all incapable of getting along, I can see only one solution. You have to smurf a civil code!

A what?

A collection of rules to smurf what's allowed and what's prohibited! That'll stop quarrels.

Everybody think about it! In three days, we'll have a general meeting to smurf on paper our Smurf Code of Good Conduct!

Smurf! They're going to end up driving me smurfy!

5

The following days, the whole village is thinking about "rules" and especially "prohibitions."

We should prohibit cutting across my field, dagsmurfit!

Prohibit smurfing any old thing in the river!

Prohibit smurfing my raspberries while walking by!

DZZRRRIIAANG

Smurfing such noise outside shouldn't be allowed!

>Whew!< Finally done...

I look awful! My hair's a mess! And my make-up is smurfed!

Hello, Smurfette!

No way! We must prohibit smurfing noses in Smurfs' homes!

I'm exhausted! Thinking about that code is smurfing!

BOOM BOOM BOOM

Say... I have some ideas to note down for the code. Can you smurf me some ink?

Grr... We must prohibit smurfing on doors at all hours!

6

The composition of the code can finally begin.

They've all arrived?

Yes, Papa Smurf! We were just smurfing for you.

It's a success, Papa Smurf. They've all smurfed suggestions!

You're exaggerating, Grouchy Smurf! If we prohibit singing, dancing, and smurfing music, we won't be able to throw parties anymore!

Me, I don't like parties!

Proposal by Lazy Smurf: prohibit smurfing noisy jobs before 10:00 a.m.

That's nonsense! Completely smurf!

But fine... To smurf my good will, I'll accept 6:00 a.m.

6:00 a.m.? You've got to be smurfing me! We have a right to sleep!

And a right to work? You smurf-for-nothing!

10:00 a.m.!

6:00 a.m.!

Okay, let's smurf 8:00 a.m. and forget about it!

Agreed.

I put the proposal to vote! Those who are for, raise your hand!

Smurfed by a two-thirds super majority. Brainy Smurf, the following proposal.

Yes, Papa Smurf!

7

The proceedings are long, very long...

Luckily, I smurfed my snack!

Z

→YAAAWN!←

You're smurfing me sleepy! Stop yawning like that!

Well, what? It's not prohibited yet!

At last, late in the night...

It's done, Papa Smurf! All the proposals have been smurfed on.

→Whew!← Finally!

Brainy Smurf and you, Poet Smurf... I smurf you the job of copying our code. And be careful about spelling smurfs!

The meeting is consmurfed! Once the code is copied, you can consult it in the library. And I'm smurfing on you to follow it!

Copying all this is going to be a smurf job!

And the work has to smurf to us...!

Oh, yes, I forgot... Out of an abundance of caution, smurf three copies of it! And most of all, get smurfing!

8

At first, everyone makes a huge effort to apply the code.

After you!

Of course not! You have the right of smurf!

Would you please repair my scythe?

Come back later! I can't smurf noise during naptime.

Are you going to smurf it in your yard?

Yes, but by following the code!

Three... four... five...

There. I'll smurf it here, six feet from your hedge.

No problem, the code's been respected!

Alas, things soon take a turn for the worse...

NO SMURFING ON THE GRASS

Lazy Smurf! Did you read what was smurfed there?

I didn't smurf on it! I crawled on it.

Don't you smurf with me! Rules are rules, and you don't smurf around with the rules! The law is smurf, but it's the law!

You know what? I don't give a smurf about your rules!

Hee hee!

13

It's outrageous, Papa Smurf! We write a code smurfcratically, and they don't respect it!

We'll have to punish them, then. Smurf them where it hurts!

You... You're going to smurf them?

No, I have another idea... At the beginning of the month, you all get a huge bag of hazelnuts. And you all like that, don't you?

Oh, yes, Papa Smurf! We adore hazelnuts!

Well then, whoever smurfs an infraction will have to pay two, three, or five hazelnuts according to the severity.

That's a smurftastic idea! They're really going to smurf about that!

Good! I name you Policesmurf. You'll note down the offenses and will smurf the penalties to them.

Papa Smurf, you know how they are... Real smurfheaded Smurfs! They'll refuse to obey me!

Smurf yourself a special outfit! An outfit that they'll recognize from a distance that smurfs respect!

Ah, yes... I could smurf the same clothes as you!

No, find something else! And now, I'd like to smurf in peace.

An outfit that's recognizable from afar... Easier said than done!

10

14

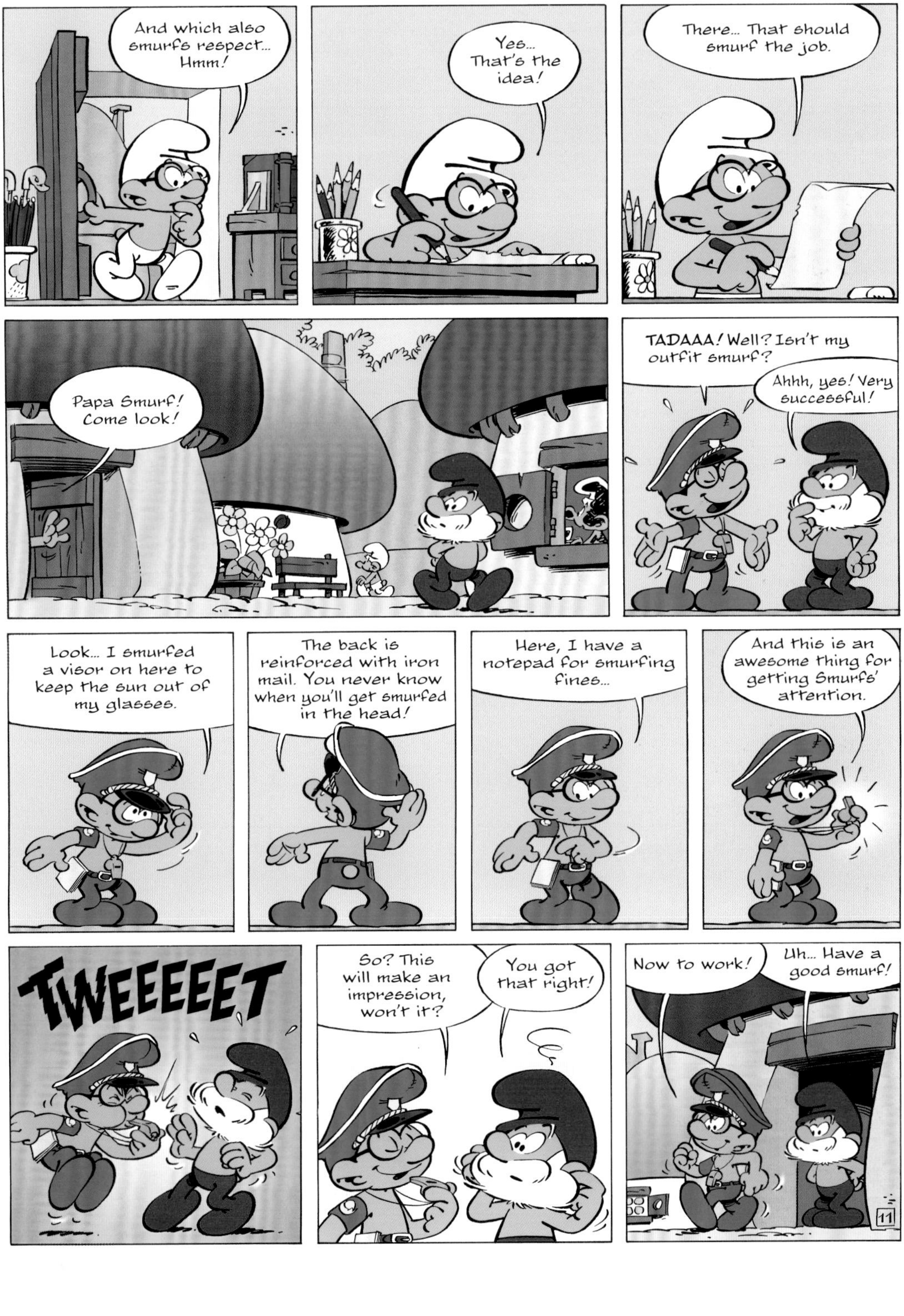
And which also smurfs respect... Hmm!
Yes... That's the idea!
There... That should smurf the job.
Papa Smurf! Come look!
TADAAA! Well? Isn't my outfit smurf?
Ahhh, yes! Very successful!
Look... I smurfed a visor on here to keep the sun out of my glasses.
The back is reinforced with iron mail. You never know when you'll get smurfed in the head!
Here, I have a notepad for smurfing fines...
And this is an awesome thing for getting Smurfs' attention.
TWEEEEET
So? This will make an impression, won't it?
You got that right!
Now to work!
Uh... Have a good smurf!
11

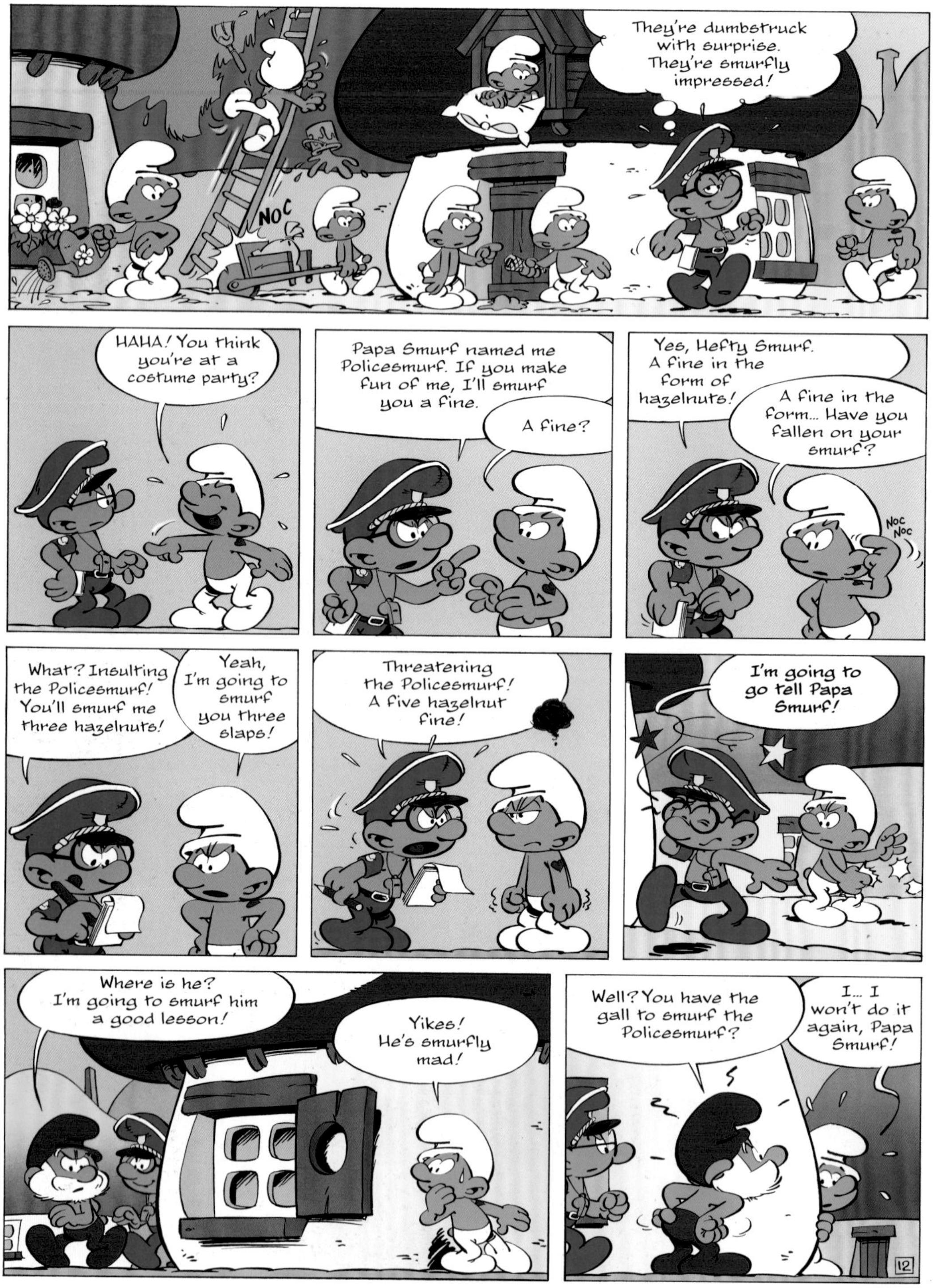
They're dumbstruck with surprise. They're smurfly impressed!
NOC
HAHA! You think you're at a costume party?
Papa Smurf named me Policesmurf. If you make fun of me, I'll smurf you a fine.
A fine?
Yes, Hefty Smurf. A fine in the form of hazelnuts!
A fine in the form... Have you fallen on your smurf?
NOC NOC
What? Insulting the Policesmurf! You'll smurf me three hazelnuts!
Yeah, I'm going to smurf you three slaps!
Threatening the Policesmurf! A five hazelnut fine!
I'm going to go tell Papa Smurf!
Where is he? I'm going to smurf him a good lesson!
Yikes! He's smurfly mad!
Well? You have the gall to smurf the Policesmurf?
I... I won't do it again, Papa Smurf!
12

 I know you won't do so again. No Smurf will do so again!

 Because I'm naming you Brainy Smurf's deputy. You'll protect him. You'll be his smurfguard!

Me? But, Papa Smurf...

 Say... If he's my assistant, I'm his boss?

That goes without saying!

 Follow me, Hefty Smurf. I'm going to smurf you a uniform!

Oh, my! I shouldn't have smurfed out of bed this morning!

 Well, I'm smurfly surprised!

 This uniform looks really good on me! It compliments my athletic shape... Doesn't it, Brainy Smurf?

 Look, Hefty Smurf. There are two hazelnuts on my armband, and one on yours!

Ah, yes. Why?

 Because my rank is higher than yours. So call me "Chief"!

 Let's go. I'll be the eyes and brains of the law, and you'll be the muscle!

Yes, Brainy Chief! Uh... Yes, Chief!

 Have you seen their smurf look?

Those two really smurf a pair!

Yes, the brute and the bootsmurf.... Ha ha!

13

17

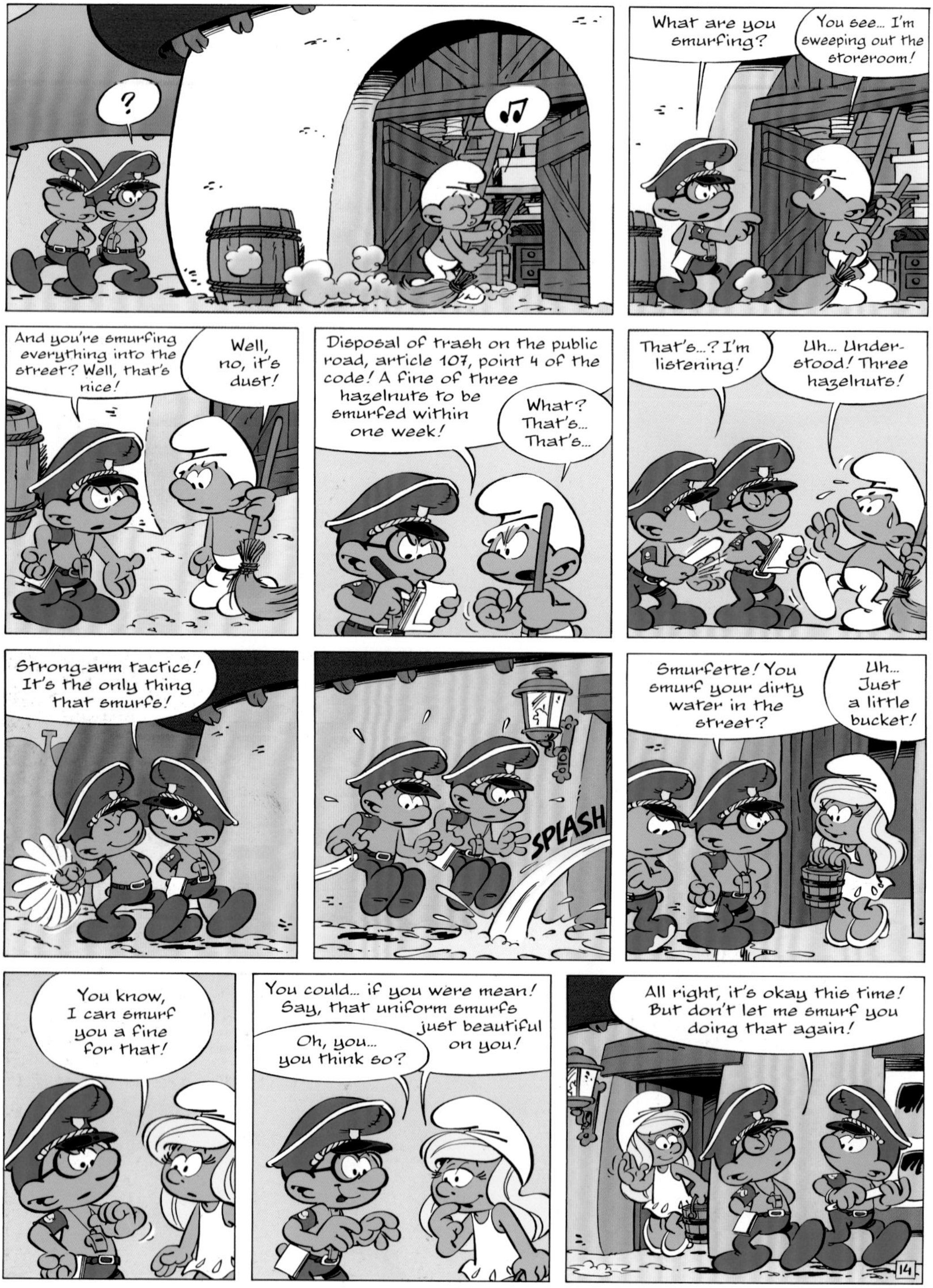
?
♫
What are you smurfing?
You see... I'm sweeping out the storeroom!
And you're smurfing everything into the street? Well, that's nice!
Well, no, it's dust!
Disposal of trash on the public road, article 107, point 4 of the code! A fine of three hazelnuts to be smurfed within one week!
What? That's... That's...
That's...? I'm listening!
Uh... Understood! Three hazelnuts!
Strong-arm tactics! It's the only thing that smurfs!
SPLASH
Smurfette! You smurf your dirty water in the street?
Uh... Just a little bucket!
You know, I can smurf you a fine for that!
You could... if you were mean! Say, that uniform smurfs just beautiful on you!
Oh, you... you think so?
All right, it's okay this time! But don't let me smurf you doing that again!
14

The two Policesmurfs work tirelessly...

TWWEEET

Here are your four hazelnuts.

I assure you this smurfs me as much as you!

FINES

PLOP

I don't know where to put all those hazelnuts anymore! I'm going to talk to Papa Smurf about it.

We could make some smurf spread with it!

Oh! What's that smoke?

Aaargh! Some air!

What's going on?

I smurfed a mistake in the amount of sulfur! But it's no big deal, it'll disperse.

No big deal? You smurf toxic, smelly substances in the atmosphere! I'm forced to--

Forced to do what?

To... to ask you firmly to smurf better attention next time!

Ah, good! Okay!

15

That's tricky.... He is Papa Smurf after all!

And this one... Look how he smurfs his cart!

What if the firesmurfs had to smurf through here! Nobody thinks about that!

A ticket! That'll cost him four hazelnuts!

For a long time, this village has been sinking into neglect and sloppiness. But believe me, that's going to change!

TWWEEEEEEE

There you go! Another poor Smurf who's going to get fined!

Hazelnuts, hazelnuts... That's all they think about!

I bet they divide them up between them as soon as your backs are smurfed!

After all, those hazelnuts are ours! We went to find them in the forest by the sweat of our smurf!

Oh, my, they're in a bad mood! Luckily, the summer fair will start soon... That will boost their smurfs!

So, my young Smurfs! Do you think this year's fair will be a success?

16

Surely, Papa Smurf! We've planned a smurftastic list full of activities!

And we'll smurf games and shows every day.

I was planning a series of meetings on the Smurf Code and its proper application!

Hmm... I think that your duties as a Policesmurf will take up all your time!

Oh, yes, that's true. Too bad!

Come. I have a little something to smurf you two!

Yes, Papa Smurf?

A series of meetings!

A close escape!

Yes... There's at least something good in this Smurf Police thing!

You're smurfing a lot of energy on a crackdown. But you also must help others! Appeal to their sympathy!

Oh! You think so?

Appeal to their sympathy... Easier said than done!

Why, there's Smurfette and our adorable Baby Smurf!

Cutcheecoo... The baby is so nice!

WAAAAH!

I think you scared him with your big smurfs!

That's a no-go, chief!

WAAAH!

17

Ah, you're just in smurf! I need help!

I've smurfed lots of cakes for the fair. But I'm afraid someone's pilfering them when I go to the storeroom...

We serve the people!

Ah, thanks!

Keep an eye on those cakes. I'll continue the patrol by myself.

Watching over cakes... Talk about a smurftastic mission!

They really do look smurfly appetizing... And I'm as hungry as a smurf!

No! I'm a Policesmurf! I must smurf my duty unswervingly!

So, no pilferer in sight?

Of course not. Not when I'm here!

Hey, what is that?

A broken plate... Why?

You threw it in with the vegetable waste. But it's not smurdegradable!

Ah, yes, that's right!

You know Brainy Smurf would smurf you a five-hazelnut fine for that?

You... You think so?

18

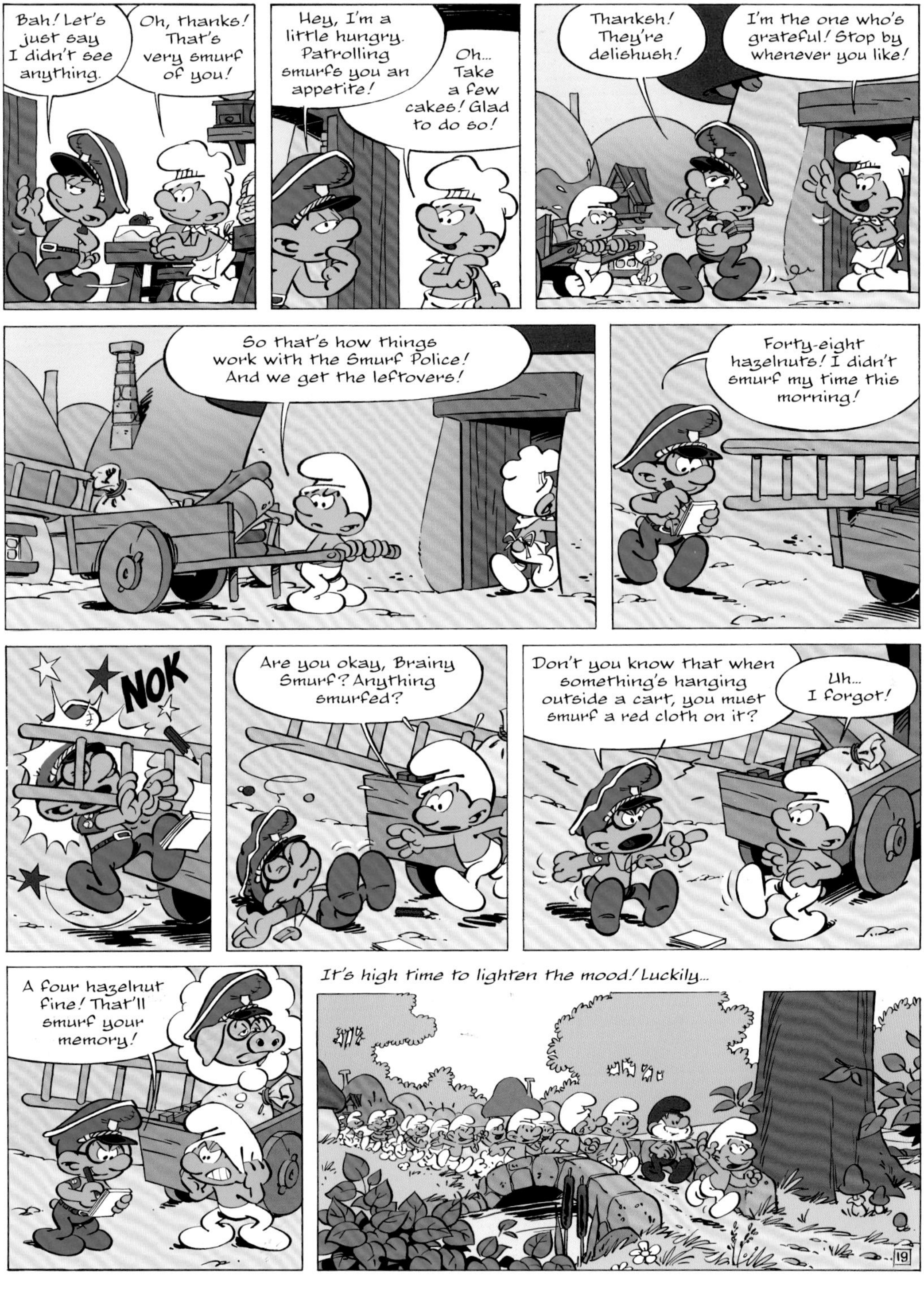

Bah! Let's just say I didn't see anything.
Oh, thanks! That's very smurf of you!
Hey, I'm a little hungry. Patrolling smurfs you an appetite!
Oh... Take a few cakes! Glad to do so!
Thanksh! They're delishush!
I'm the one who's grateful! Stop by whenever you like!
So that's how things work with the Smurf Police! And we get the leftovers!
Forty-eight hazelnuts! I didn't smurf my time this morning!
NOK
Are you okay, Brainy Smurf? Anything smurfed?
Don't you know that when something's hanging outside a cart, you must smurf a red cloth on it?
Uh... I forgot!
A four hazelnut fine! That'll smurf your memory!
It's high time to lighten the mood! Luckily...
19

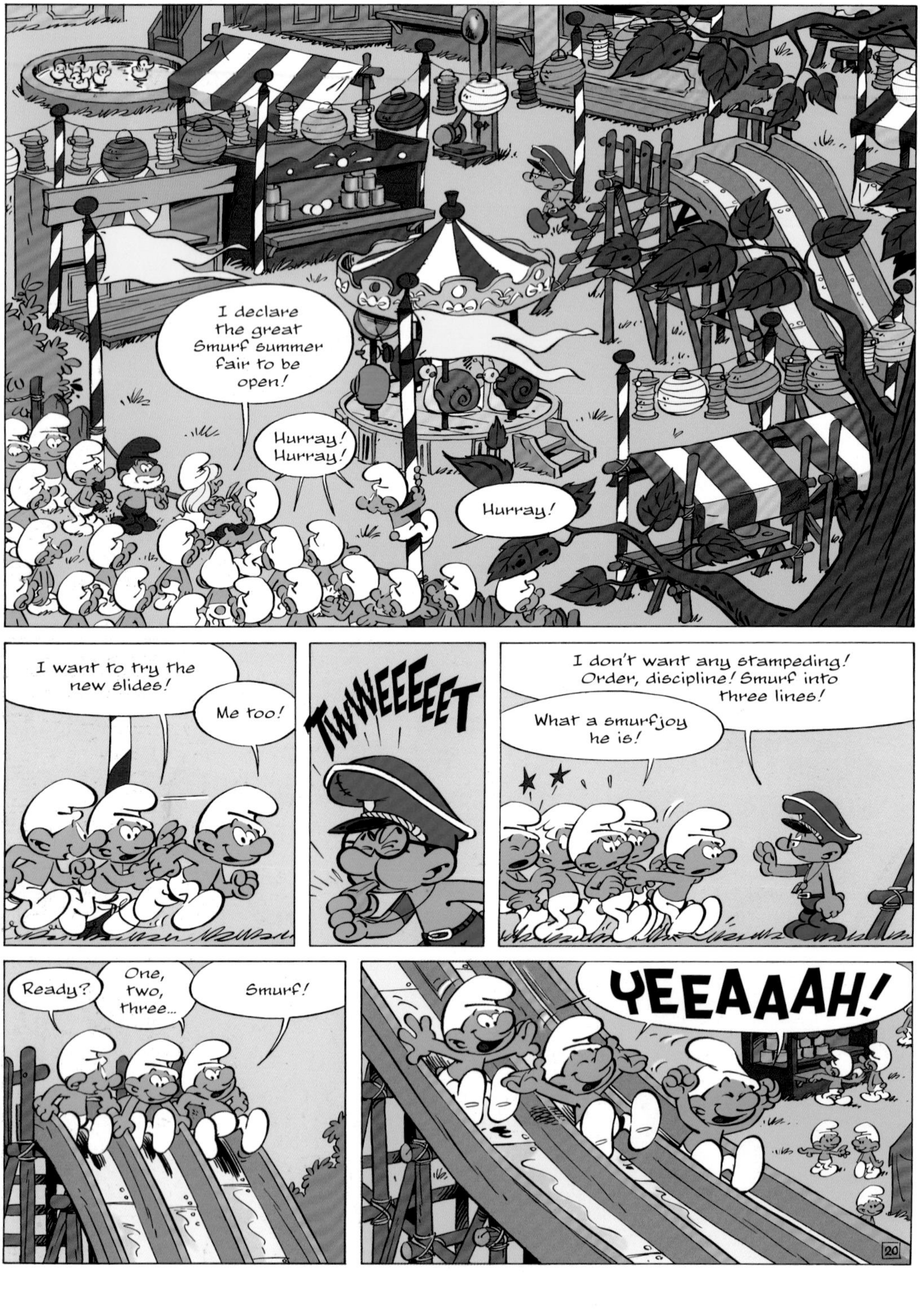

I declare the great Smurf summer fair to be open!
Hurray! Hurray!
Hurray!
I want to try the new slides!
Me too!
TWWEEEEEET
I don't want any stampeding! Order, discipline! Smurf into three lines!
What a smurfjoy he is!
Ready?
One, two, three...
Smurf!
YEEAAAH!
20

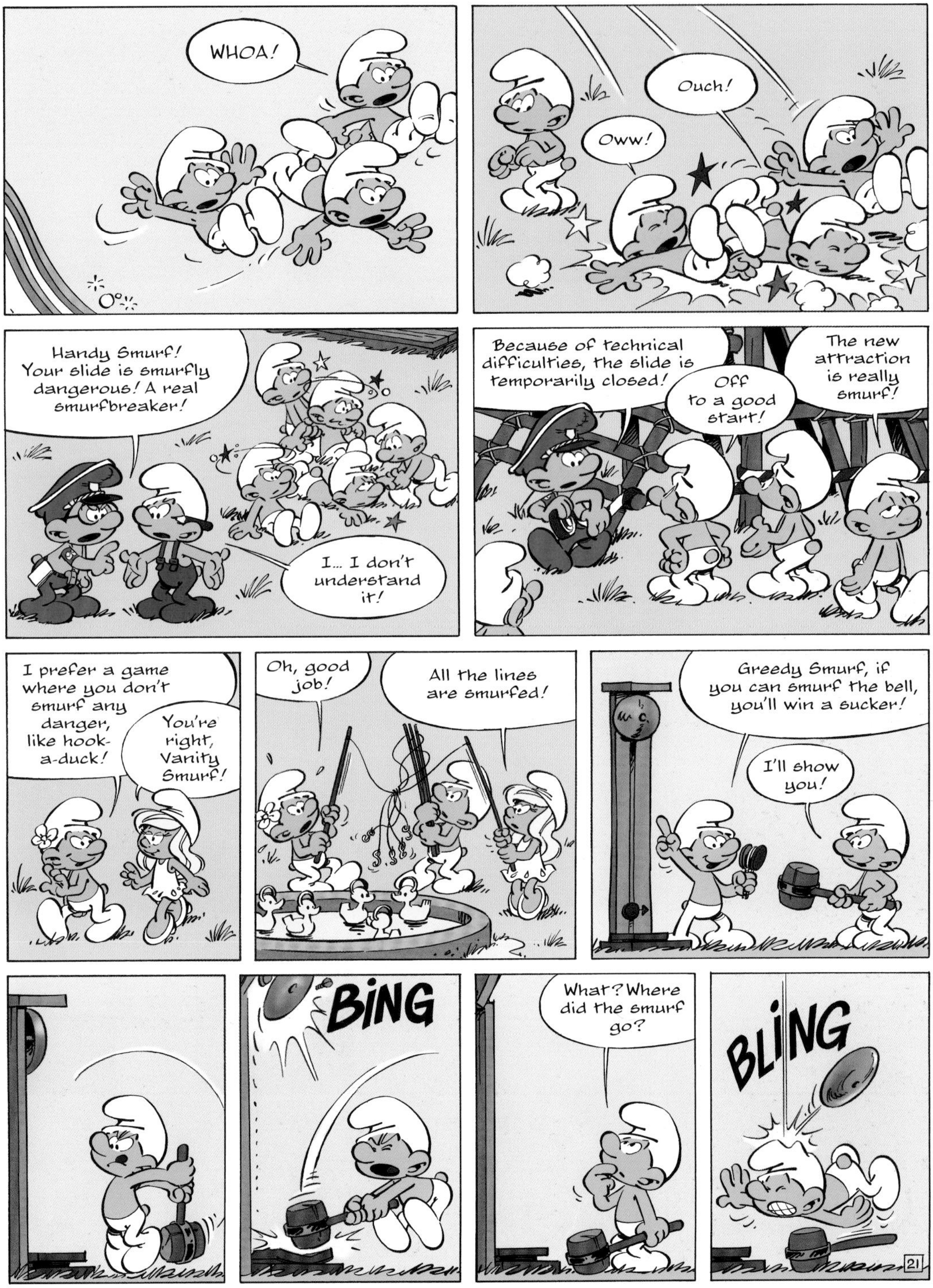
WHOA!
Ouch!
Oww!
Handy Smurf! Your slide is smurfly dangerous! A real smurfbreaker!
I... I don't understand it!
Because of technical difficulties, the slide is temporarily closed!
Off to a good start!
The new attraction is really smurf!
I prefer a game where you don't smurf any danger, like hook-a-duck!
You're right, Vanity Smurf!
Oh, good job!
All the lines are smurfed!
Greedy Smurf, if you can smurf the bell, you'll win a sucker!
I'll show you!
BING
What? Where did the smurf go?
BLING
21

Hey, here are two suckers... It rang twice!

I... I didn't smurf how strong I was!

Soap! Someone smurfed soap everywhere!

And raised the end! So obviously they're going to smurf off!

What a shocking joke! Jokey Smurf has smurfed too far this time!

Jokey Smurf! Where are you?

Here!

I'm going to have a huge bump! That slide is a real smurfery!

Strange! If he's one of the victims, he's not the one who smurfed that trick. But who then?

This fair is badly organized!

Yes! Everything's smurfing wrong!

I think it's time to smurf the rest of the schedule!

The tug-of-war contest will smurf soon... We're waiting for the teams!

You don't stand a chance, you pack of smurfs!

We don't? We're going to smurf you a good lesson!

22

Ready? Set...

Smurf!

SMURF!

Let's go, they're on their last smurfs!

Brace yourselves, Smurfs! They're gonna crack!

SNAP

HEY!

Noc

Oh, nice job!

Well, smurf!

Where did you smurf that rotten rope?

Uh... The contest is canceled. We'll smurf to the sack-race right away!

THE

This shouldn't smurf any problems at least!

I hope the sacks are solid!

The rope was smurfed with a knife! There were only three strands left!

The situation is smurf! We're dealing with a saboteur!

A saboteur? Are... Are you sure?

Absolutely! But have no fear. It won't take me long to collar him!

23

27

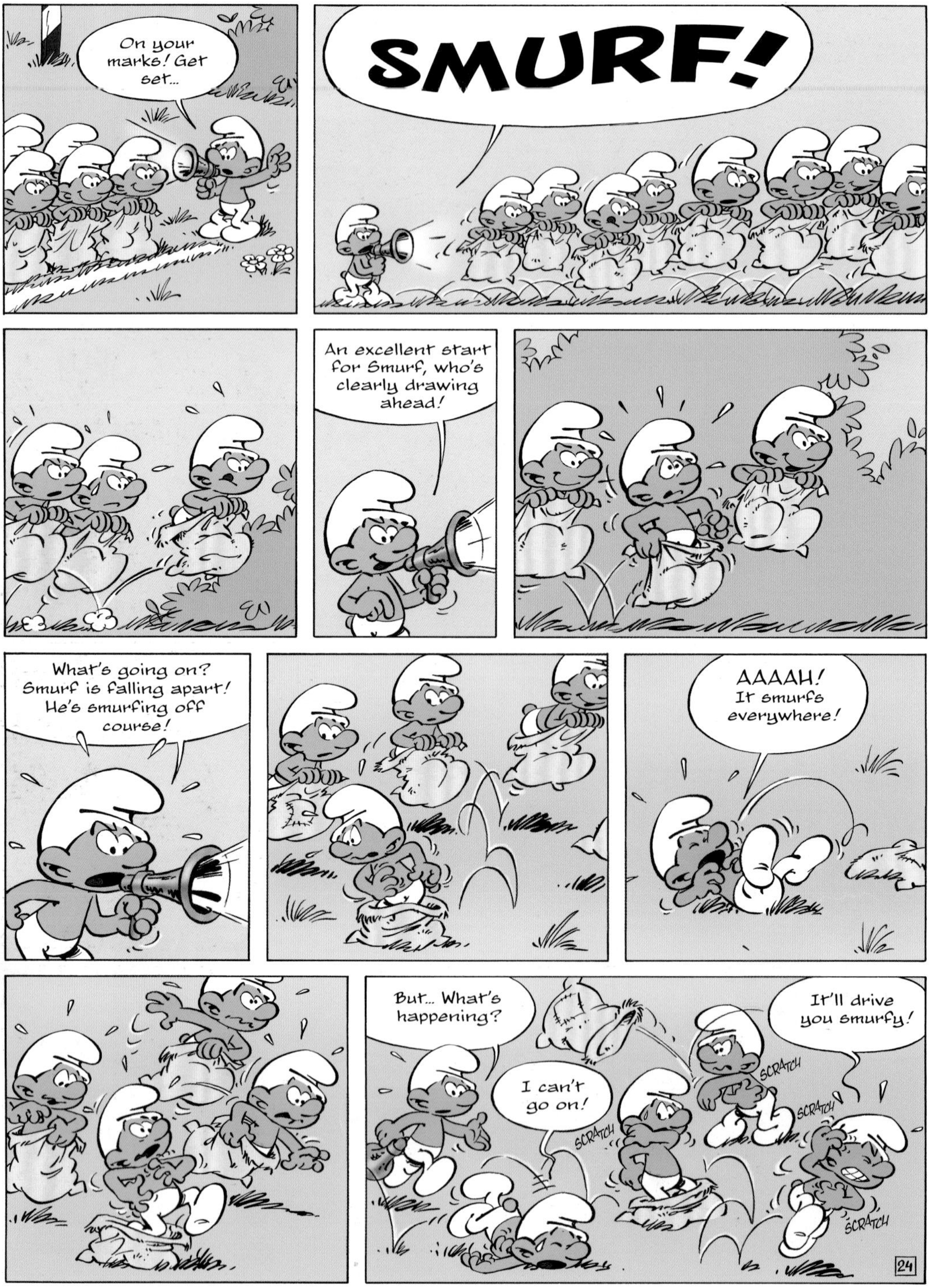
On your marks! Get set...
SMURF!
An excellent start for Smurf, who's clearly drawing ahead!
What's going on? Smurf is falling apart! He's smurfing off course!
AAAAH! It smurfs everywhere!
But... What's happening?
I can't go on!
SCRATCH
It'll drive you smurfy!
SCRATCH
SCRATCH
SCRATCH
24

The duck pool!

Aaaaah!

That smurfs crazy good!

Someone smurfed itching powder in the sacks!

That blasted saboteur is smurfing with us!

The news spreads very quickly...

A saboteur among us? No way!

The Policesmurfs said so!

Everyone becomes suspect...

And mistrust reigns.

Are you sure nobody smurfed any pepper in that?

When things finally settle down...

I'm 542 years old and have rheumatisms. Who am I?

BOMBOMBOMBOMB

?

What? The show is starting already?

BOM
BOM
BOM

No way! The performance of "The Smurfs of the Round Table" is tomorrow!

But yes, look... The curtain is smurfing!

The Smurfs of the Round Table

25

CREEEEEEEE

For smurf's sake! He's taunting us!

Quick, smurf a walk around the stage! He may be escaping through the back!

Nobody here...

So?

Not a Smurf in sight!

He must have mingled with the others after smurfing the curtain!

The paint was just put on... It's still running!

Nobody smurf from here! And everybody, raise your hands!

What?

Has he fallen on his smurf?

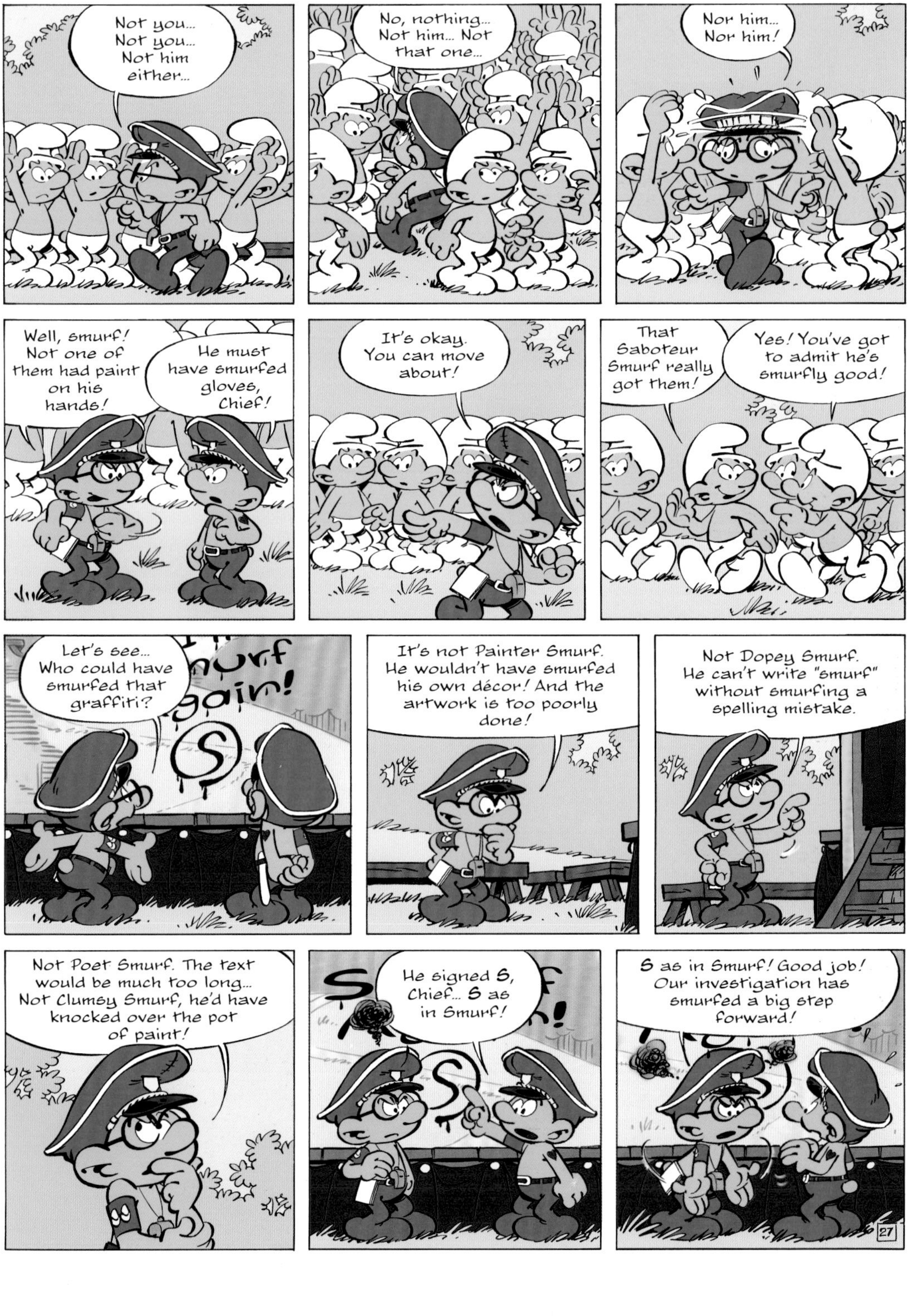

Not you... Not you... Not him either...
No, nothing... Not him... Not that one...
Nor him... Nor him!
Well, smurf! Not one of them had paint on his hands!
He must have smurfed gloves, Chief!
It's okay. You can move about!
That Saboteur Smurf really got them!
Yes! You've got to admit he's smurfly good!
Let's see... Who could have smurfed that graffiti?
It's not Painter Smurf. He wouldn't have smurfed his own décor! And the artwork is too poorly done!
Not Dopey Smurf. He can't write "smurf" without smurfing a spelling mistake.
Not Poet Smurf. The text would be much too long... Not Clumsy Smurf, he'd have knocked over the pot of paint!
He signed S, Chief... S as in Smurf!
S as in Smurf! Good job! Our investigation has smurfed a big step forward!

Let's see instead if he didn't smurf a clue behind him!

Ah! That's smurfly interesting! By jumping down from the stage, he smurfed a good print from his right foot on the ground!

We especially mustn't ruin it! Go find Handy Smurf. And tell him to bring some plaster!

Yes, Chief!

There... It'll be dry in a few minutes!

I want you to smurf a perfect casting.

We just have to compare this print to that of every Smurf in the village!

What do they want now?

I don't know.

Z

They're starting to smurf on our nerves!

Smurf your foot in there!

Huh? Why?

That smurfs perfectly! You're the saboteur!

What? You've fallen on your smurf!

What's more, it's not my size! That's smurfing my big toe!

Hmm!

Okay. Your turn!

28

It's exactly right this time! We've got him!

One moment! Smurf your foot in the print yourself!

Me? But I'm the Policesmurf!

So what? That doesn't smurf you above the law!

That fits exactly!

We've smurfed the saboteur!

How was I to know Smurfs all have the same feet?

Smurfette is innocent, in any case!

At the fair...

So? Is the investigation going in circles?

Obviously... It's more complicated than smurfing us with fines!

Our reputation is at stake! We have to smurf something else.

?

He wrote that he would smurf again. When? Under cover of night, of course.

So, we'll smurf watch on the fairgrounds all night long if we have to!

All night long? But, Chief...

No "buts"! We have to smurf him in the act!

Okay, okay! I'll go fix a snack...

That night...

With two, we should be able to keep the whole fair in our smurf of vision! I'll smurf there under the flap.

I'll smurf myself behind the panel! I'll be able to see without being seen.

Perfect. Keep your eyes peeled!

But keeping watch is tiring...

And a night is a long time!

ZZZ

ZZZ

CRAC

Huh?

Halt! Don't move!

BONK

Oww! What an impact!

TWEEEEET

30

Huh? What? Coming, Chief!

STAND STILL!

Nobody!

It can't be... He smurfed right from under our noses!

I bet you were asleep! You should be ashamed!

Yes, Chief. Sorry, Chief.

What's more, he had time to smurf another dirty trick!

We'll have to inspect the entire fair with a fine-toothed smurf!

There's no need, Chief. I found it!

31

Go find some scissors! We have to smurf them into pieces before someone sees them!

Honestly, Chief... It's not a strong resemblance!

There... We have nothing further to smurf here. Let's go sleep a few hours.

Yes, Chief. I'm worn out!

Later...

He's driving us smurfy, Papa Smurf. I'm starting to lose hope.

By provoking him in turn, we could smurf a trap for him. But how?

I have a plan to propose to you. But you have to smurf me all the hazelnuts that you've collected!

?

That afternoon, the fair resumes...

Listen up! The Smurf Police invite you into their tent!

They'll smurf all your questions concerning the Smurf Code!

⇒Pfft!⇐ What an attraction!

The code! Always the code!

32

You can also taste their delicious hazelnut cream!

That's much more interesting!

They definitely owe us that. They took the hazelnuts from us!

The invitation from the Smurf Police is a resounding success.

This hazelnut cream is delicious!

And it seems it helps intestinal smurf!

Good timing, I feel a little bloated.

How surprising, Greedy Smurf!

But Hefty Smurf remains on the lookout.

Nothing still?

No. Maybe he won't dare smurf anything today?

There will be hazelnut cream for everyone. We smurfed a whole barrel of it!

TCHIRP
TCHIRP
TCHIRP

Listen... A little bird must have smurfed under the tent!

Hmm... That bird has a weird song!

TCHIRP
TCHIRP
TCHIRP

I'll run and smurf a look, Chief!

Smurf out of my way!

Hey! Careful there!

That noise was smurfing from the rear...

TCHIRP
TCHIRP
TCHIRP

I've smurfed you this time!

Hey?!

PLAF

It's him, Chief! The saboteur!

TWWWEEEEET

Darn! He slipped right from under our smurfs again!

NOOOO!

Missed him! I'm going to have a nervous smurfdown!

He's escaped us once again, Papa Smurf! It's a total bust!

Maybe not... I smurfed a little trick of my own on him.

34

I sprinkled the barrel's surroundings with a liquid of my making. He had to have smurfed in it.

As it evaporates, that product smurfs little shiny crystals. The saboteur will leave some behind him!

I don't see anything, Papa Smurf!

I expected that... So, I smurfed you this!

Thanks, Papa Smurf! You were right. I see crystals!

And here are others... He smurfed in this direction!

The trail is smurfing towards the village!

There's no doubt. He crossed the bridge!

Aha! We're going to smurf him now!

It's a smurftastrophe! I don't smurf anything now. The trail is gone!

Maybe this way, Chief?

You're right. I see traces smurfing straight towards that door!

35

He's in the storeroom!

Do I bust in the door?

Yes, we'll smurf him by surprise!

Don't move! You're smurfed!

For smurf's sake! He's trying to get away again!

I'm coming!

He's done laughing at us this time!

And we'll finally find out who he is!

What? It's... it's you, Smurf?

?

Huh? He's the saboteur?

I'd never have guessed!

It's unbelievable! Such a lowkey Smurf!

Exactly! I'm fed up with being a lowkey Smurf!

Grouchy Smurf, Greedy Smurf, Dopey Smurf... All of them are popular! And even that good-for-nothing Lazy Smurf!

Whoa! A little respect!

But nobody smurfs any attention to me! Nobody hardly recognizes me! And you all just call me Smurf!

36

And yet, who brings the lanterns for parties? Who puts them away afterwards? Who repairs them? Me! But nobody smurfs!

That's right. You're the one who does all that!

But "Smurf who brings out the lanterns for parties and puts them away afterwards" is kind of long for a name!

I'm known when it comes to smurfing me fines! I sweep the shed, park my cart, transport material... Each time, they smurf me!

Oh? That was always you?

I didn't notice!

But some Smurfs avoid the fines... Smurfette, Chef Smurf who gives away cakes... And Papa Smurf, of course!

Hmm...

That's true! It's always the little folk who get smurfed on!

If I understand right, you're frustrated because nobody pays attention to you except to smurf you fines. You think that you've experienced injustices and you tried to get revenge by provoking the Policesmurfs!

But he sabotaged the fair!

We were given fines, too!

That's no reason for annoying everyone!

Did you hear that? I'd like to give you a pass this time... If you promise to stop your smurferies!

I... I promise!

To smurf you a lesson, you'll go without hazelnuts until winter!

So, let's forget about that! Tomorrow, there will be a dance and a fireworks show. I want everyone to smurf a good time.

You're smurfing off easy, Frustrated Smurf!

What? I don't want to be called Frustrated Smurf!

37

The next day, calm seems to have returned. However...

What was he smurfing in the storeroom again?

That Lantern Smurf doesn't inspire any trust in me. I'm smurfing an eye on him!

Oh! Flames!

Quick, I must...

PSSSSSHH

Alert! All the rockets are going to smurf!

Oh, the lovely smurf!

Shut up, Dopey Smurf!

Go get the fire-cart! And all the buckets you can smurf!

The explosions finally stop.

I don't think there are any rockets left. Let's go in!

38

The struggle against the fire is long and painful.

Finally, at day's end...

It's all put out, Papa Smurf!

The damage is serious!

Yes, the storeroom is half smurfed!

But... How did this fire start?

Lantern Smurf is surely the one who smurfed the fire!

Me? You're crazy!

Don't try and smurf me! You left the storeroom in a hurry... Then I saw the flames!

But I didn't smurf anything bad! I was going home, that's all!

Think! Maybe you smurfed a lit candle behind?

No, no, nothing was burning! I'm innocent, Papa Smurf!

Liar! You're a smurfomaniac, an arsonist!

You've gone stark raving smurf!

We shouldn't have trusted you!

We're going to smurf you a lesson!

Yeah!

Calm down, calm down! You're not going to smurf anything at all! It's late, and we're all exhausted. We'll talk about this again tomorrow!

It may be too late by tomorrow!

Yes! What if he smurfed something else bad?

You'll understand that, as a suspect, I must smurf you into detention. Policesmurfs, lock him in his home!

At home won't smurf anything. He can escape!

He must be smurfed in prison!

But we don't have a prison! This is no longer the times of Smurfissimus.

I have an idea, Chief!

Let me out! This is an abuse of my Smurf rights!

I can't take being locked up! I have smurfophobia!

BOM
BOM

AAAH!

I WANT OUT!

I have to smurf away and fast!

Lantern Smurf! Are... Are you running away?

40

44

I don't want to be locked up anymore! But I'm innocent, Smurfette! I smurf you my word.

I'd like to believe you. But...

Then, go tell Papa Smurf! He must help me prove my innocence!

Here, go smurf the prisoner something to eat!

Yes, Chief!

For smurf's sake!

ALERT! HE'S ESCAPED!

I have to run! I'm going to smurf in the woods!

Smurfette, you haven't seen Lantern Smurf?

Uh... No, Hefty Smurf!

Then, smurf your door tightly! He could be dangerous!

Look everywhere. We have to find him!

I must talk with Papa Smurf. I promised.

41

He fled into the woods, but he says he's innocent. This story is becoming smurfly strange!

And the others smurfing all over to find him They're not about to calm down.

Tomorrow morning, we'll examine the storeroom. We must smurf the key to this mystery before things take a bad turn.

In the meantime, go sleep. We can't smurf anything further for the moment!

Until tomorrow, Papa Smurf!

HALT! Who goes there?

It's me!

You shouldn't be outside with Saboteur Smurf prowling around! Go home quick!

We're going to smurf rounds all night long in case he's cooking up a dirty trick.

Yes! The Smurf Police are outmatched. We must smurf things into our own hands!

Lantern Smurf was right to go into the woods. He's safer there!

HOOHOO!

42

The next day...

Hmm!

Aha! I'm starting to understand what smurfed!

At what time did the fire start?

Uh... Three in the afternoon. I was about to smurf myself a cup of herbal tea.

Three o'clock! That's just what I thought!

We must resmurf the scene. Let's go find Lantern Smurf!

You're going into the forest? Be careful about Saboteur Smurf!

Don't you smurf about us!

Yoohoo! Where are you?

Lantern Smurf? It's me, Papa Smurf!

He's not showing himself! Where could he have smurfed?

Here!

EEEEEEEEEE!

Listen to me... If we want to smurf proof of your innocence, you must return to the village with us!

If you say so, Papa Smurf!

Well, smurf! They've captured him!

He's going to eat and rest. This afternoon, we're going to resmurf the scene of his arrest.

Of his arrest after the fire?

No, of his first arrest!

Frankly, I don't see what that would smurf!

Me either, Chief. We know he's guilty!

That afternoon...

You, go into the storeroom. You'll smurf everything like the other day!

Yes, Papa Smurf!

So! How did the arrest take place?

Well, I was smurfing his trail, with my magnifying glass in hand...

Hey! Where did I smurf that magnifying glass?

That doesn't matter. Go on!

The traces smurfed straight towards the storeroom...

I smurfed the door a big kick!

When he saw us, he tried to smurf out the window. He struggled...

I intervened and helped Hefty Smurf to get control of him!

With one hand?

Huh? Why do you smurf that?

48

You were holding your magnifying glass!

My magnifying glass... That's right. I must have smurfed it somewhere!

Ah, there it is! It's in that pot!

NO! Don't touch anything!

Let's go back to yesterday's fire. At what time did you see the first flames smurfing?

Uh, well... At this time, I think?

No, it had to have been a few minutes later. We must wait!

But... What difference does that smurf?

There! At this precise hour, the sun smurfs straight through the skylight.

Ah yes, that's true! So what?

Now, observe closely what smurfs!

What smurfs?

Frankly, I don't understand!

Nothing at all is sm--

Oww!

Well, smurf! That burns!

My magnifying glass! My magnifying glass is what smurfed fire to the box of rockets!

What? You're the arsonist?

That's smurfer than smurf!

I told you so! I'm innocent!

45

It's your fault, too! You were smurfly suspect!

My fault? You're not ashamed to say that?

Yes, you're right! I... I smurf you my humblest apologies, Lantern Smurf!

Yeah, fine! You could've thought about that sooner!

Papa Smurf, I no longer feel worthy to smurf my duties as a Policesmurf. I resign! Here's my whistle.

Uh... Are you sure?

I resign, too, out of solidarity with the Chief! I'll smurf you my billy club.

Okay! Who volunteers to replace them?

Uh... Not me!

Me either. That job's no everyday smurf!

What if we all smurfed an effort to respect the code?

Good idea! We could make do like before, without the Smurf Police!

Yes... But if there's a disagreement still, what do we smurf?

WE'LL GO TO PAPA SMURF'S HOME!

At least I tried... But you can't escape your fate!

That evening, the fair's closing dance is a big success... with no police presence and no saboteur!

It's too bad there won't be any fireworks!

Me, I don't like fireworks!

Me either!

THE END

46

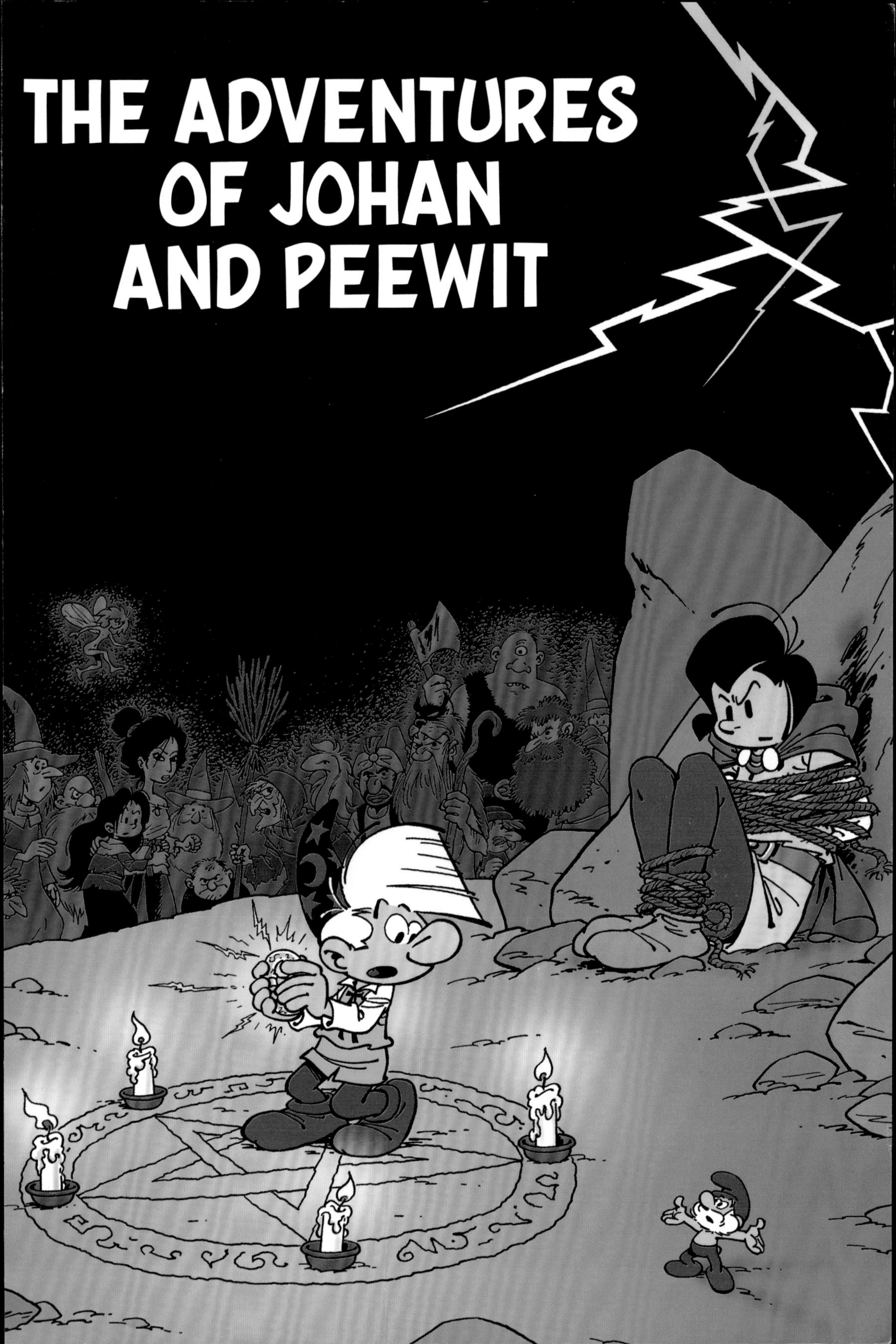
THE ADVENTURES
OF JOHAN
AND PEEWIT

THE NIGHT OF THE SORCERERS

The Night of the Sorcerers

The first sunbeams pierce the fog of Charcoal Forest.

But, Johan, is it really necessary for us to go through here?

It's the shortest way, Peewit. What's worrying you?

People say there are sorcerers around here! I don't want to be turned into a toad! Also, it stinks of sulfur fumes!

Ha ha! You still believe in those old wives' tales!

The fumes are from the charcoal burners!

But there aren't any charcoal mines out here!

No, you big doofus! Charcoal is made out of wood. It doesn't come from "coal" mines.

You have to burn wood under a pile of dirt to--

AAAAH!

4

Kind Lord...

Would you kindly help an old woman carry her heavy bundle of wood to her wretched cottage?

Why, of course, my good lady.

No, Johan, don't go!

Come on, Peewit! A little politeness! Where must I carry your wood, Ma'am?

It's nearby, Milord, and you're very generous.

Poor Johan! She's probably going to bewitch him with her claw-like fingers and viperous look.

And what will become of me, all alone in this forest full of enchantments?

Oh, Johan, why didn't you listen to me? Now you're the victim of that creature's spells, maybe you've already been devoured by her--

What are you saying, Peewit?

2

Honestly, Peewit, you're exaggerating! You see witchcraft everywhere!

A very kind young man, indeed! He placed all the wood that I had there... I'll return the favor one day!

As for the other one, the little one, I wish for him to get hiccups!

Ɫɯɨʃɑɯ oʄ ʋɨɣɫɯɟɡʔ Ƨɨɨ Ɫɯɑɯɨɾɨ'ɫɨ?

?

HIC!

You were saying, Peewit?

And now HIC I've caught HIC the HICcups! Scare me, Jo HIC!

If you like, we can go back in the forest...?

No, no thank you. I'm already much better!

3

55

A few hours later...

...And here we are at Master Homnibus's home!

Do you think he still has that awesome raspberry liqueur?

Please, Peewit, behave better than the last time!

Me? I misbehaved? ME?!

The liqueur, Peewit! The last time, going home, we had to tie you to Annie because you couldn't keep yourself upright!

It's not my fault if Annie drank too much!

Master Homnibus! It's me, Johan!

...And Peewit!

MASTER HOMNIBUS! IT'S US!

BOM BOM

No answer... He must have gone on a trip!

It's too bad... Such a yummy raspberry drink.

Good riddance!

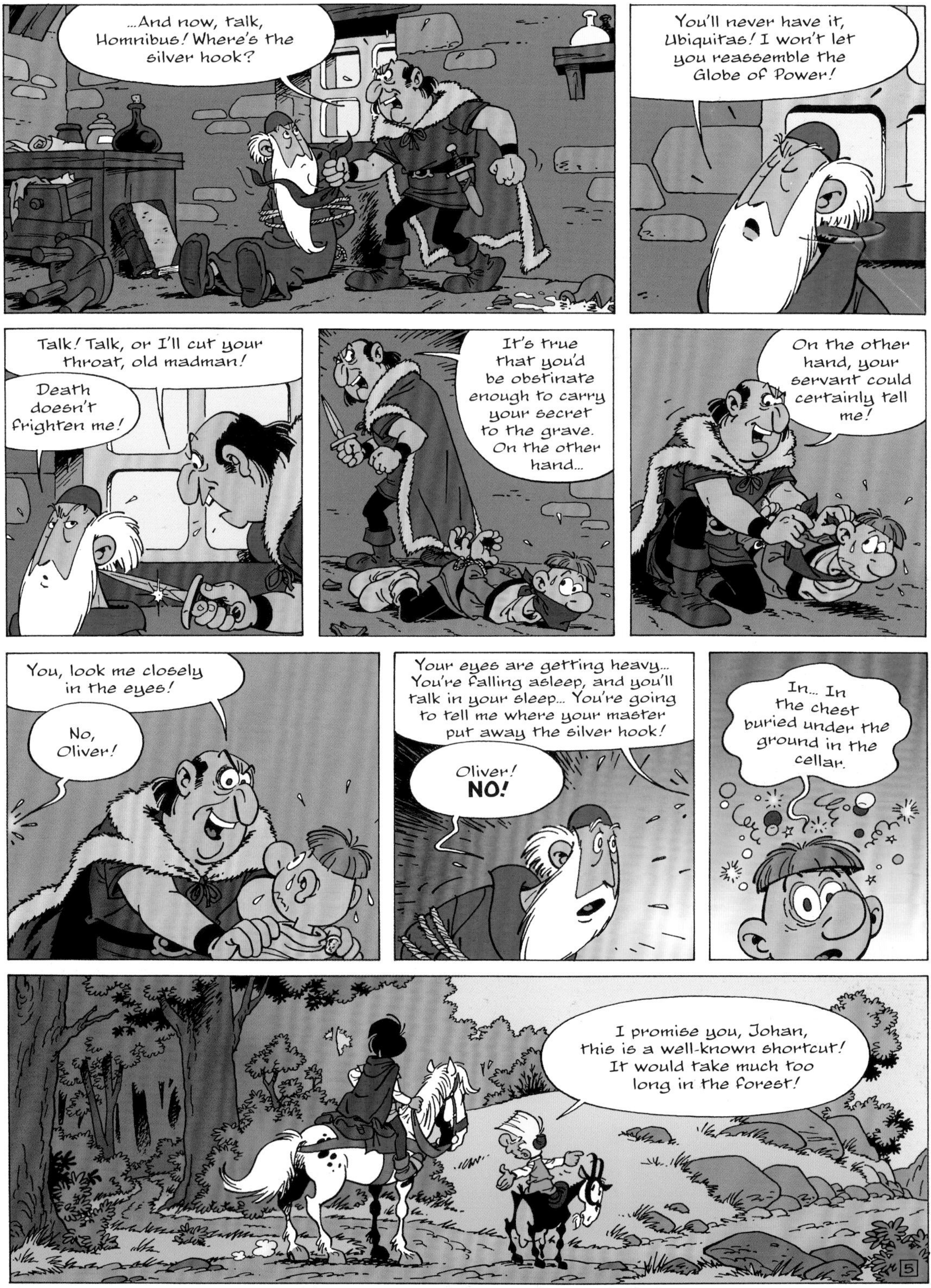
...And now, talk, Homnibus! Where's the silver hook?
You'll never have it, Ubiquitas! I won't let you reassemble the Globe of Power!
Talk! Talk, or I'll cut your throat, old madman!
Death doesn't frighten me!
It's true that you'd be obstinate enough to carry your secret to the grave. On the other hand...
On the other hand, your servant could certainly tell me!
You, look me closely in the eyes!
No, Oliver!
Your eyes are getting heavy... You're falling asleep, and you'll talk in your sleep... You're going to tell me where your master put away the silver hook!
Oliver! NO!
In... In the chest buried under the ground in the cellar.
I promise you, Johan, this is a well-known shortcut! It would take much too long in the forest!
5

No way, Peewit. This is the path that's way too long. You're just scared of going back into the forest, that's all!

Scared, me? Hahaha! What a laugh!

It's simply that I think the forest air is unhealthy because of all those fumes and sorcerers...

So you prefer the air in the Devil's Bite Pass.

!?
Devil's Bite? What's that?

The pass that we're entering. People say that, once, a peasant saw--

AAAAH!

?
Johaaan!

Johan! Another witch!

Calm down, Peewit! You see that you scared her!

Don't worry about my companion, Miss. He's not dangerous!

We mean you no harm!

And what's with all that?

We'll catch her!

Little devil girl!

Let's get her!

Did you see the young witch go by?

The... The little girl there? Well...

What do you want with her?

She's a cursed witch!

Since she arrived, barns and haystacks have been going up in flame all by themselves!

And she's causing the livestock to die!

Spoiling the milk!

Since she got here, my rheumatism has been making me suffer horribly!

Yes! That young Amandine is a witch! Just like her mother, Miriam! They must die!

I know where their hideaway is in the Boar Forest. Let's all go there together and make them pay for their misdeeds!

YES!

Death to them!

We'll burn them!

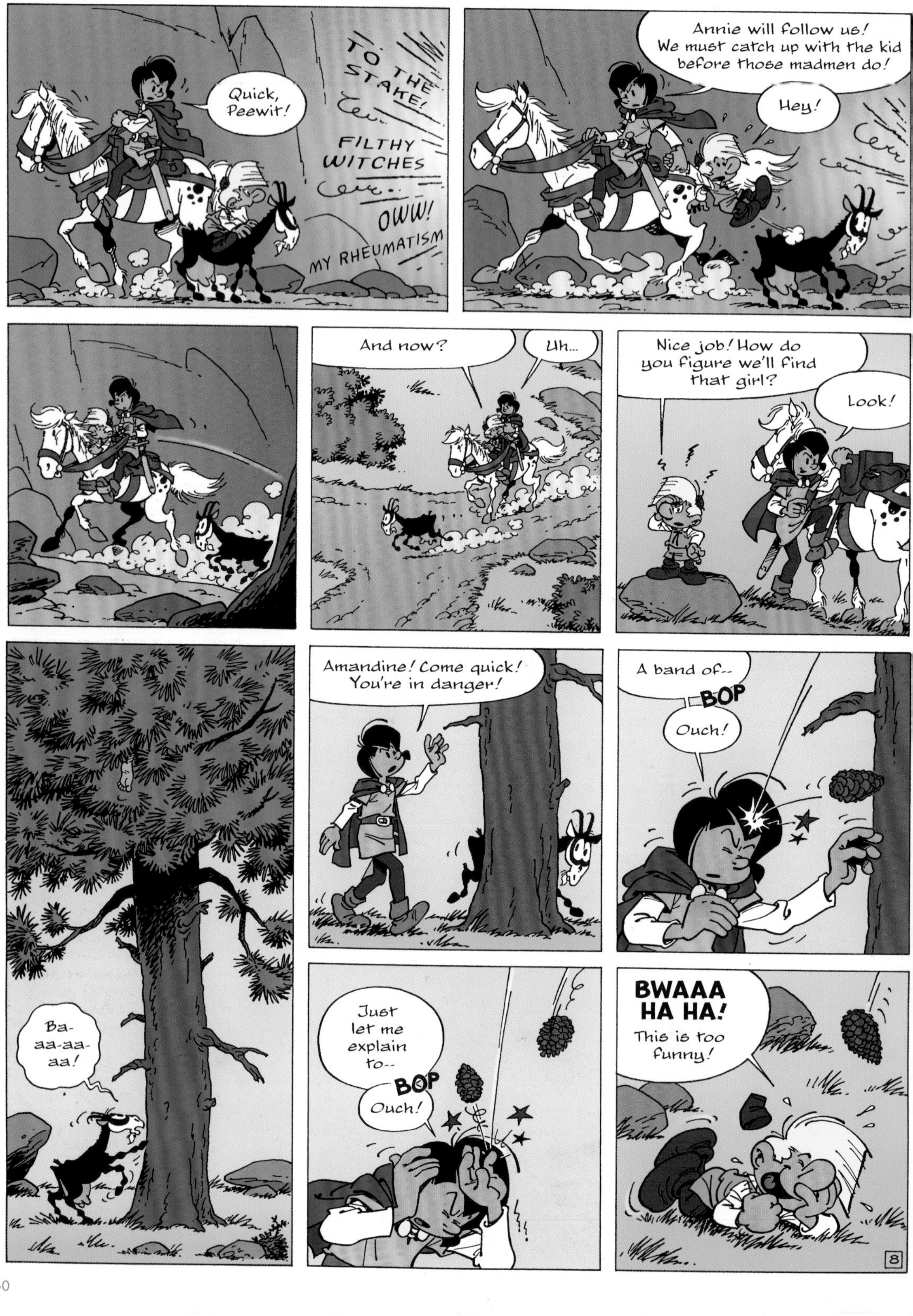
Quick, Peewit!
TO THE STAKE!
FILTHY WITCHES
OWW! MY RHEUMATISM
Annie will follow us! We must catch up with the kid before those madmen do!
Hey!
And now?
Uh...
Nice job! How do you figure we'll find that girl?
Look!
Ba-aa-aa-aa!
Amandine! Come quick! You're in danger!
A band of--
BOP
Ouch!
Just let me explain to--
BOP
Ouch!
BWAAA HA HA! This is too funny!
8

HA! HA! HA!

BOP

Ouch!

?! Hey... the other one... Where did he go?

Eeeeeee!

Amandine, we have no time to lose! You and your mother are in great danger!

My mother? But... How...?

The peasants are looking for you! A man in purple says he knows where you live!

In purple? That slimeball Ubiquitas!

There's not a moment to lose!

There she is! She has accomplices!

There!

We've got her!

Sic her!

Death!

Oowee! My rheumatism!

I know where they're going. Follow me!

9

Careful! There's a bramble barrier! We'll have to continue on foot here!

Now I'll have to blindfold you. I promised Mom I'd never reveal the path to our house to anyone.

Awesome! We come to save her, and she wants to play blind man's buff!

Stop it, Peewit. It's up to her to keep her promise.

And now, bend over and come this way.

It's a secret path that Mama devised.

Ouch! It's full of brambles through here!

We'll be there soon!

And this blindfold is so tight you can't take it off!

Of course! It's a witch's knot!

A WITCH?!

Oh!

So, what have you dragged home, Amandine?

Ma'am, I'm Johan, the king's page, and my companion's name is Peewit. We've come to warn you of a great danger!

A great danger, really? And what's that, pray tell?

A group of peasants is searching for you! They want you dead!

Young man, know that I am the great Miriam, the fabulous magician who knows all the secret powers and doesn't fear a bunch of imbeciles armed with pointy sticks!

Yes, Mom, but Ubiquitas is the one leading them!

Ubiquitas? What the devil! This is serious, then...

11

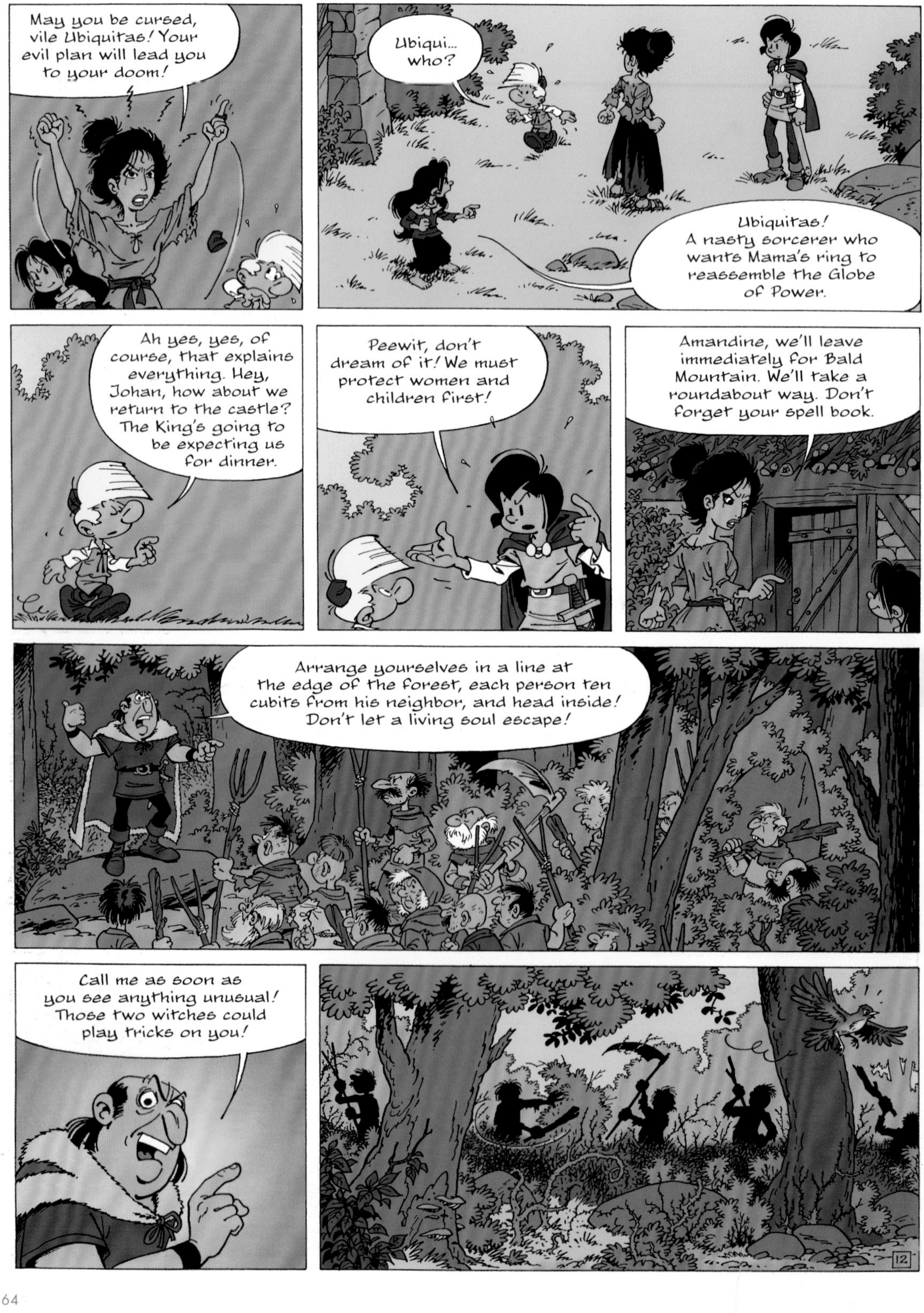
May you be cursed, vile Ubiquitas! Your evil plan will lead you to your doom!
Ubiqui... who?
Ubiquitas! A nasty sorcerer who wants Mama's ring to reassemble the Globe of Power.
Ah yes, yes, of course, that explains everything. Hey, Johan, how about we return to the castle? The King's going to be expecting us for dinner.
Peewit, don't dream of it! We must protect women and children first!
Amandine, we'll leave immediately for Bald Mountain. We'll take a roundabout way. Don't forget your spell book.
Arrange yourselves in a line at the edge of the forest, each person ten cubits from his neighbor, and head inside! Don't let a living soul escape!
Call me as soon as you see anything unusual! Those two witches could play tricks on you!
12

The wind is blowing from the east... Perfect!

Amandine, douse these cloths in the benzoin vinegar, then give them to our guests.

It's to protect your nose and mouth.

Mom's going to make a fire of Morpheus vine shoots.

g'eꞇꞇowi om bio ꝑꞅ 6ꞇyꝏꝑꝏꝑꝺ ꝑꞅ mꝺꝛyꝓꝺꝙ'

Is that understood? At the slightest suspicious sign, call out!

Hey, tell me, Odilon, who's this lord who's commanding us?

I haven't a clue, Lucas. He just turned up to help us with witches.

That Milord doesn't seem very easy-going! He scares me...

Hey, do you smell that odor?

SNIF SNIF

My goodness... Feels like...

...I'm going to have a little nap!

⇒YAWWN!⇐

SNRRRFL

SNRFL

13

The sleeping smoke must have produced its effect by now! Let's go!

Follow me!

There's no point blindfolding you now. After the night on Bald Mountain, I'll never come back here again!

There! There they are!

14

CAPTURE THEM!

Faster, Annie! That fellow doesn't look very trustworthy!

She's escaping me! Miriam is escaping me! RRAAH! I'm exploding with rage!

PSSHOOFF

?!
?
?!

Let's go the length of the forest. That'll be stealthier!

PSSHOOFF

So, Miriam? You thought you could run out on me?

15

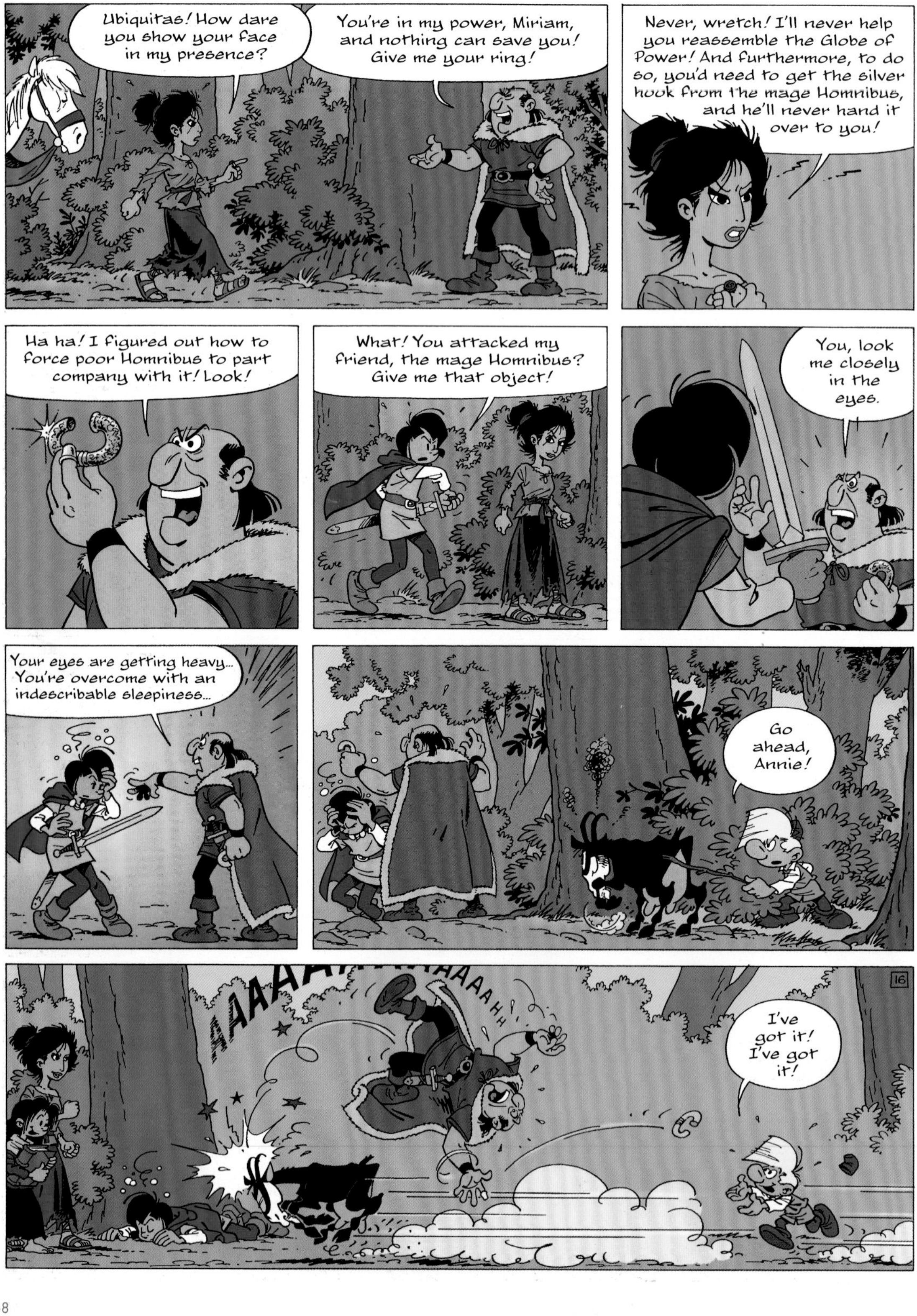
Ubiquitas! How dare you show your face in my presence?
You're in my power, Miriam, and nothing can save you! Give me your ring!
Never, wretch! I'll never help you reassemble the Globe of Power! And furthermore, to do so, you'd need to get the silver hook from the mage Homnibus, and he'll never hand it over to you!
Ha ha! I figured out how to force poor Homnibus to part company with it! Look!
What! You attacked my friend, the mage Homnibus? Give me that object!
You, look me closely in the eyes.
Your eyes are getting heavy... You're overcome with an indescribable sleepiness...
Go ahead, Annie!
16
I've got it! I've got it!

What... What happened?

Let's not stay here. That man is dangerous.

I have the... Master Homnibus's thingy!

You're escaping me again, Miriam! And with the silver hook! But I'll get my revenge!

Later...

We'll have to cross over the Cursed Pass before nightfall... Then we can stop off at a place that I know.

Even later...

But say, Amandine, what's that thing that was stolen from Master Homnibus?

The silver hook? Look, it's written here...

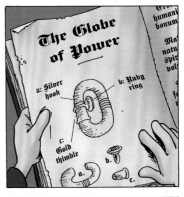

The Globe of Power

a: Silver hook
b: Ruby ring
c: Gold thimble

The Globe of Power would give enormous powers to whoever possesses it. That's why nobody can possess the three parts at the same time. The ring was entrusted to Mom, the hook to Master Homnibus...

...And, unfortunately, the gold thimble is in the possession of that swindler Ubiquitas!

But we should've taken it from him while he was knocked out!

No way! We'd have had the three pieces together, and that's forbidden!

Too bad! Enormous powers!

What? No light at Master Homnibus's home? But it's the evening when we smurf our chess match.

Maybe he went smurfing, Papa Smurf... Or he's sick... Or he forgot... Or...

We'll find out very soon, Brainy Smurf!

Strange... There's not even a fire in the hearth.

Pa... Papa Smurf!

PAPA SMURF! COME HELP US QUICKLY!

?!

And that scoundrel Ubiquitas smurfed the silver hook?

His plan is clear: he means to reassemble the Globe of Power and use it during the night on Bald Mountain!

But that's horrible! That smurf-for-nothing would then hold absolute power over the entire universe of magic!

SMAK

We absolutely must warn the sorceress Miriam! Without a doubt, he's going to go after her, too!

I'll smurf there immediately! Come, my young Smurfs!

18

The sorceress Miriam lives in a clearing in the Boar Forest! You'll find her easily from above, Papa Smurf!

FLAP FLAP FLAP

CRAck

!

Odilon!? What are you doing here in the dead of night?

The same thing as you, Eusebius! I've come to see whether there isn't any treasure hidden in the witches' house!

But I've searched everything. There's nothing left!

I'm uneasy... If the witches find us here, they might cast a spell on us!

There's no danger! They were seen heading towards Hanged Man's Pass!

We've heard enough, my young Smurfs! We'll head off again for Hanged Man's Pass!

There! A stork! In the dead of night!

It's a sign of bad luck-- let's get out of here!

FLAP FLAP

19

Later...

Here's Hanged Man's Pass, my young Smurfs... No trace of Miriam! And I doubt she could've gotten so far in such a short time.

Let's head back. We won't find anyone here.

Dawn already! We have to get going again!

RRR

≈YAWWWWWWWN!≈ What an idea, getting up so early!

We must if we want to arrive at Bald Mountain in time!

Bald Mountain? But what will we be doing there?

One night a year, all mages and sorcerers gather there for their secret ceremony. That's where I'm going to take my sorcerer's apprentice examination.

Oh? Maybe I could become a sorcerer, too! Because, hey, I know a thing or two!

You boil some bat-milk over a fire of mandrake roots and then--

One moment!

?

20

Starting from here, three paths can take us to our goal. The first one follows the crest of the hills, the second one passes through a village, and the third crosses through the forest.

Let me concentrate!

At the same instant...

A whole herd of chamois?

A half-dozen at least. They're going to drink at the spring near the path to the hills.

A good catch on the horizon!

PSSHOOFF

? ? ?

Look into my eyes.... Your eyelids are getting heavy...

Listen to me closely. A witch heading to Bald Mountain may pass by this way. You're going to capture her.

If needed, you'll kill her along with those accompanying her and wait till I come back.

PSSHOOFF

21

At the same instant, too...

≈YAWWWWWN!≈ Now that I've finished my night watch, I'm going to go have a nap.

Me too. Besides, nothing ever happens here at this time of the day...

PSSHOOFF

Look into my eyes...

A witch may pass over this bridge. Kill her if necessary, along with those accompanying her, and wait for me.

PSSHOOFF

Still at the same instant...

PSSHOOFF

Look into my eyes...

I see danger in the hills and near the village... Let's take the path that goes through the forest!

...And so, a decoction of spider web with a fragment of stork nest lets whoever drinks it fly in the air like a bird...

Yikes!

Whoa!

Ayyyyy...

...

Anything broken, Peewit?

No, I don't think so... I wonder...

If you shouldn't add a flake of butterfly wing...

Let's not dawdle. We have to be at Bald Mountain before nightfall!

HELP ME!

It's just ahead of us!

MERCY!

LET ME GO! I HAVEN'T DONE ANYTHING!

The man in purple told us to capture you and wait for him!

MERCY!

And to kill you, if need be.

What are you doing there? Let that old woman go!

Kind Lord, save me from these madmen!

The man in purple said so!

Ubiquitas! Him again!

If you touch a hair on her head...

It's no use, Johan. They can't understand anything. Ubiquitas has cast a spell on them.

Peewit! Come help me!

There's no point, Johan! Lady Miriam will get you out of this!

There's a way to restore their consciousness...

Ah! We're going to see some real magic! If it were me, I'd cast a spell with blood from a black hen killed on the day of a full moon--

Look out!

PSWEEEEEEEEEET!

Huh... What am I doing here?

Who are these people?

An intense noise was needed to snap them out of their trance.

Thank you, Ma'am, and you, kind Lord. I'll repay you for that.

Come now, you poor old lady. What could you do for great and mighty sorcerers like us?

25

Let's not dawdle here, my friends. We're expected on Bald Mountain for the big sorcery gathering.

Sorcerers!

They're sorcerers!

Let's get out of here!

I'll knock that little smart aleck down a peg or two!

Peewit, you shouldn't have talked like that in front of the lumberjacks. Sorcerers aren't well-liked in this area.

HIC!

We must warn the village of sorcerers passing through. We have to keep them from coming near our homes.

Sorcerers bring bad luck!

PSSHOOFF

⁉

What are you doing here? I gave you orders to capture a witch!

Gave orders, eh? Hey, you there, you wouldn't be a bit of a sorcerer, by any chance?

Look into my eyes...

26

78

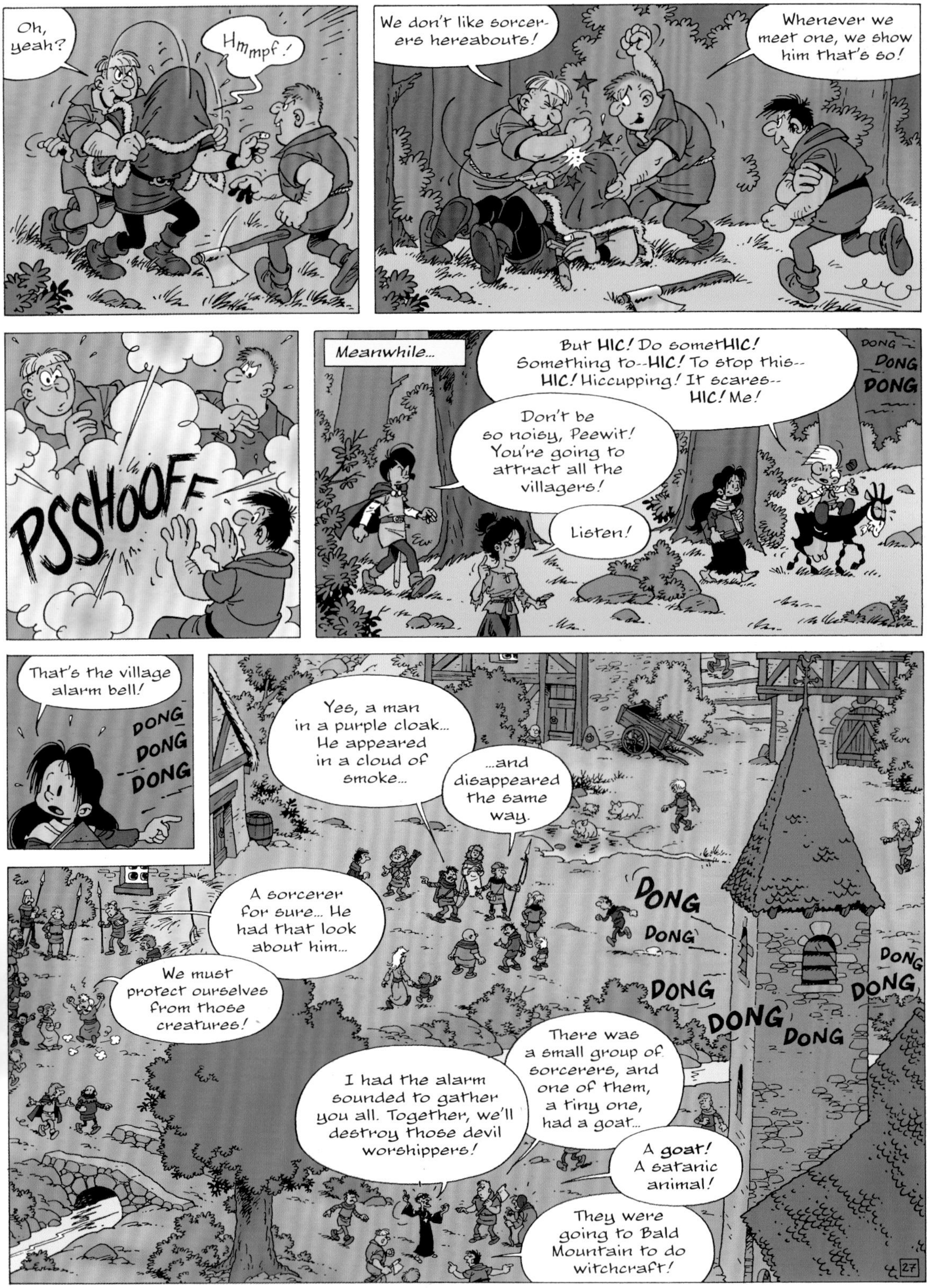
Oh, yeah?
Hmmpf!
We don't like sorcerers hereabouts!
Whenever we meet one, we show him that's so!
PSSHOOFF
Meanwhile...
But HIC! Do sometHIC! Something to--HIC! To stop this--HIC! Hiccupping! It scares--HIC! Me!
DONG DONG DONG
Don't be so noisy, Peewit! You're going to attract all the villagers!
Listen!
That's the village alarm bell!
DONG DONG DONG
Yes, a man in a purple cloak... He appeared in a cloud of smoke...
...and disappeared the same way.
A sorcerer for sure... He had that look about him...
We must protect ourselves from those creatures!
DONG DONG DONG DONG DONG DONG DONG
There was a small group of sorcerers, and one of them, a tiny one, had a goat...
I had the alarm sounded to gather you all. Together, we'll destroy those devil worshippers!
A goat! A satanic animal!
They were going to Bald Mountain to do witchcraft!
27

We must crush the devilry all around us. It's threatening us!

Heaven commands it!

Let's annihilate those creatures!

And to start with, let's track down those heading towards Bald Mountain. They can't be far away!

Hic!

Hic!

Hic!

HIC!

Let's leave this path and cut through the woods. We'd do best to avoid any bad run-ins.

Hic!

Can't you do anything for Peewit, Mom?

We're coming into the lands of the Hublinbu Ogre... There will surely be an occasion to frighten him!

HRRROOAARRR!

28

80

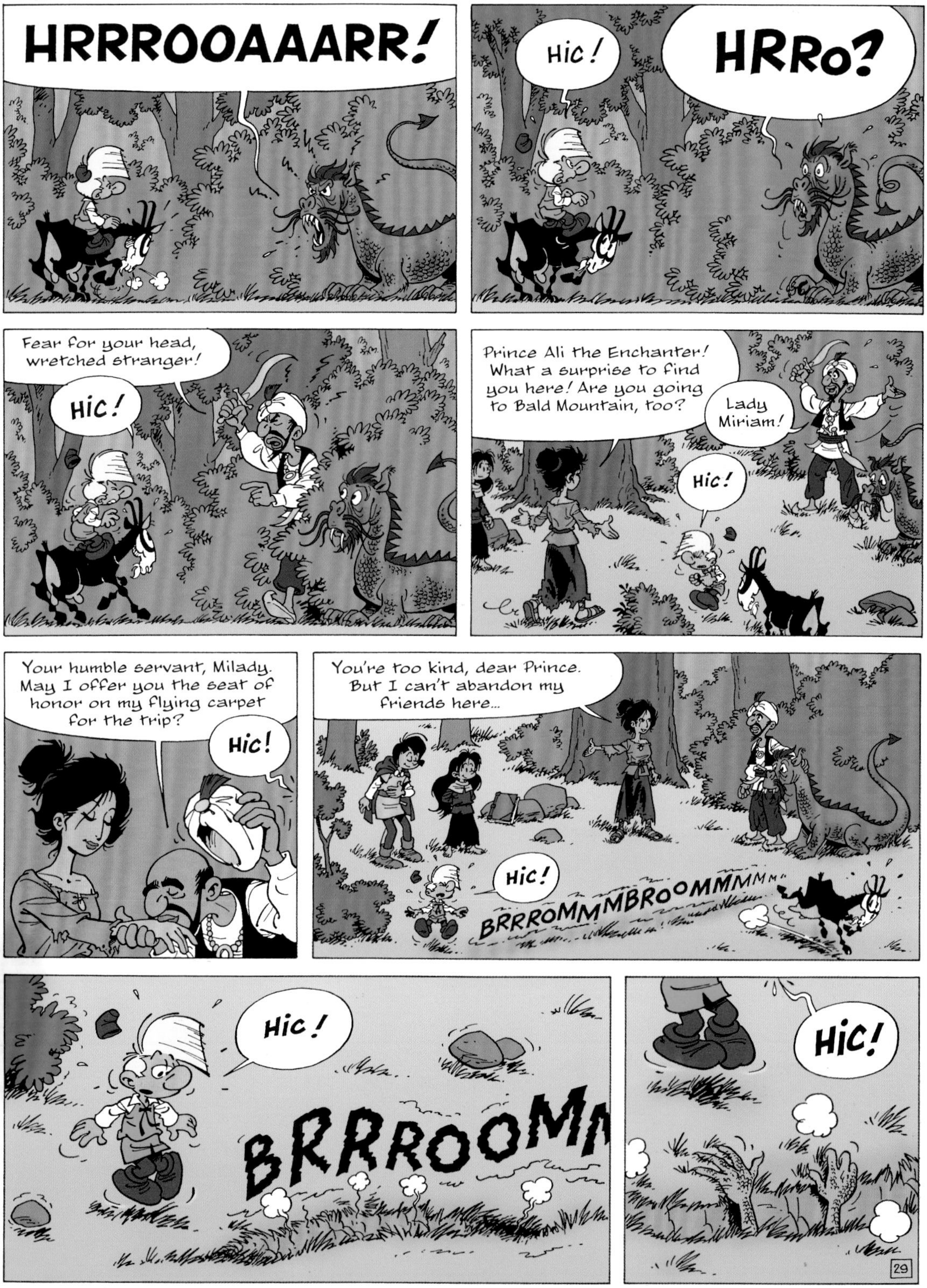

HRRROOAAARR!
Hic!
HRRo?
Fear for your head, wretched stranger!
HIC!
Prince Ali the Enchanter! What a surprise to find you here! Are you going to Bald Mountain, too?
Lady Miriam!
Hic!
Your humble servant, Milady. May I offer you the seat of honor on my flying carpet for the trip?
Hic!
You're too kind, dear Prince. But I can't abandon my friends here...
Hic!
BRRROMMMBROOMMMMM
Hic!
BRRROOMM
HIC!
29

Vat isss all thisssss?

HIC!

Oh! Hello, Madam Wyvern! We haven't seen one another in so long!

Amandine! Goodnesss me! I vassn't esssspecting to ssssee you here!

HIC!

Tonight will clearly be an important meeting! How are you doing, my dear?

HIC!

HIC! And mean--HIC! Meanwhile--HIC! Nobody's taking--HIC! Care of my--HIC! Hiccups--HIC!

?

Hoho! What's this that I see here?

A little boy! I'm crazy about little boys. Especially roasted on a skewer! Hahahaha!

HIC!

!

Hang on, Peewit! I'll get you out of this!

No, Johan!

Milord Ogre, let that young man go, please. He's one of us.

30

82

Oh, sorry, Lady Miriam! I didn't know he was one of your children...

HIC! I'm not--HIC! a child--HIC! I'm HICteen years--HIC old!

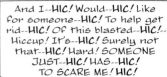

And I--HIC! Would--HIC! Like for someone--HIC! To help get rid--HIC! Of this blasted--HIC!--Hiccup! It's--HIC! Surely not that--HIC! Hard! SOMEONE JUST--HIC! HAS--HIC! TO SCARE ME! HIC!

Be careful, Peewit, there's a spider on your sleeve!

What? Where? Where?

I can't stand those things!

Stop squirming around like that! Now it's climbing towards your ear!

SOMEBODY GET IT OFF ME!

Oh! Nice job! Now it's going down your shirt collar!

BAM BAM

AAAHH! HELP ME!

There. We can leave again now. His hiccups is cured.

HA! HA! HA! Hee hee hee!

If that was a joke, it's not funny at all!

Meanwhile, at the home of the mage Homnibus...

...And we looked everywhere, Master Homnibus. But if Lady Miriam went through the forest, we won't be able to spot her.

ELIXIR

31

There's only one thing left to do: go to Bald Mountain myself!

Master, don't think of it! You're in no condition!

Do you have the whips? The ropes? The nets? The crosses? Let's go! Before tonight, the Evil One's worshippers will be roasting at the stake!

So, they're heading that way? Towards Bald Mountain?

Then their path will have to pass over the Old Bridge!

No, I'm sorry, I can't stay with you much longer. I sense a danger drawing near. We must cross the Old Bridge before night!

Oliver is right, Master Homnibus. Bald Mountain is far from here.

Yes, Master! You'd have to ride horseback for hours...

I absolutely must foil the plans of that traitor Ubiquitas and warn Lady Miriam... If it's not too late already!

But where will we find a horse fast enough? And a cart?

I won't go via the road. I'll take the Garter Snake River.

The... The river... But that's an even longer trip what with all those twists and turns! And you'd have to go against the current! And it's fast! And—

Hand me the big atlas, Oliver!

32

PFFF... Are you sure, Master Homnibus, that...

Master Homnibus, I don't smurf how you could...

Look here, rather!

We just have to go down the Garter Snake River...

But Bald Mountain is in the opposite direction!

...And here, we'll cross to the other bank. Next to the Count Onme Meadow, we'll go afloat again and will go down river to Woodland Forest...

Understood!

Master Homnibus

Noisu Brook

Garter Snake River

Mistletoe Oak

Woodland Forest

Count Onme Meadow

Carefree Summit

Doityurself Cliff

Helpme Chapel

Old Hag Grottos

Bronze Falls

Lake Ata

Bandit Rivulet

Feelfine Torrent

Bald Mountain

Garter Snake Stream

Once there, we'll cross the strip of land to get to the river again and go downriver to Carefee Summit...

Carefree Summit

...And so on, by following the current to the Doityurself Cliff, then we'll cross without getting our feet wet and rejoin the river, which goes down towards the Helpme Chapel...

We'll be at Bald Mountain before the end of the night!

But... But we don't have a boat...

We have something better, Oliver! Follow me!

33

This will get us out of this fix!

?

Travelers' accounts gave me the idea of building this out of reeds and leather.

NO ENTRY

NO ENTRY

A... A leather boat?

Yes, and I'm certain it can't sink!

We're going to put it in the water, too.

The Old Bridge is only a quarter of a league away, but I sense that danger awaits us there. We'd do better to cross the river here.

A bridge? There's a bridge a little farther along?

Peewit! Where are you going?

By the time you've climbed up the other side, I'll have caught up with you! And with dry feet!

Hide in the underbrush! We'll have to capture the sorcerers by surprise!

Faster, Annie! We have to be on top of the cliff before them!

Hey, there's that old lady again! We certainly do run into her everywhere!

34

Someone's coming! Be ready!

Hey... What's going on there?

Bandits are attacking the poor old lady! Faster, Annie!

Hey there, peasants! Let that pretentious old bag go!

That's him! I recognize him! The sorcerer with a goat!

!?

Seize them, too!

The first one who touches me...

Ouch!

BING

POW

BIFF

NOC

BOOM

Now we have something to break in our stake!

Say, Milord, wouldn't the goat be better on a grill?

35

Return to the village, my young Smurfs! I'll go with the travelers.

Are... Are you sure we won't sink like a stone?

There's no danger, brave Oliver! We're off to Bald Mountain!

!?

What's that?

My word! Peewit is a prisoner!

I'm going to rescue him!

Wait, Johan!

Light this once you're above them.

It will make your job easier!

Look out! Someone's trying to surprise us!

I don't see how the light of a candle can help me.

CLIC CLIC CLIC

What the--?

I can't see a thing!

Ah! Now, I understand!

More devilry!

36

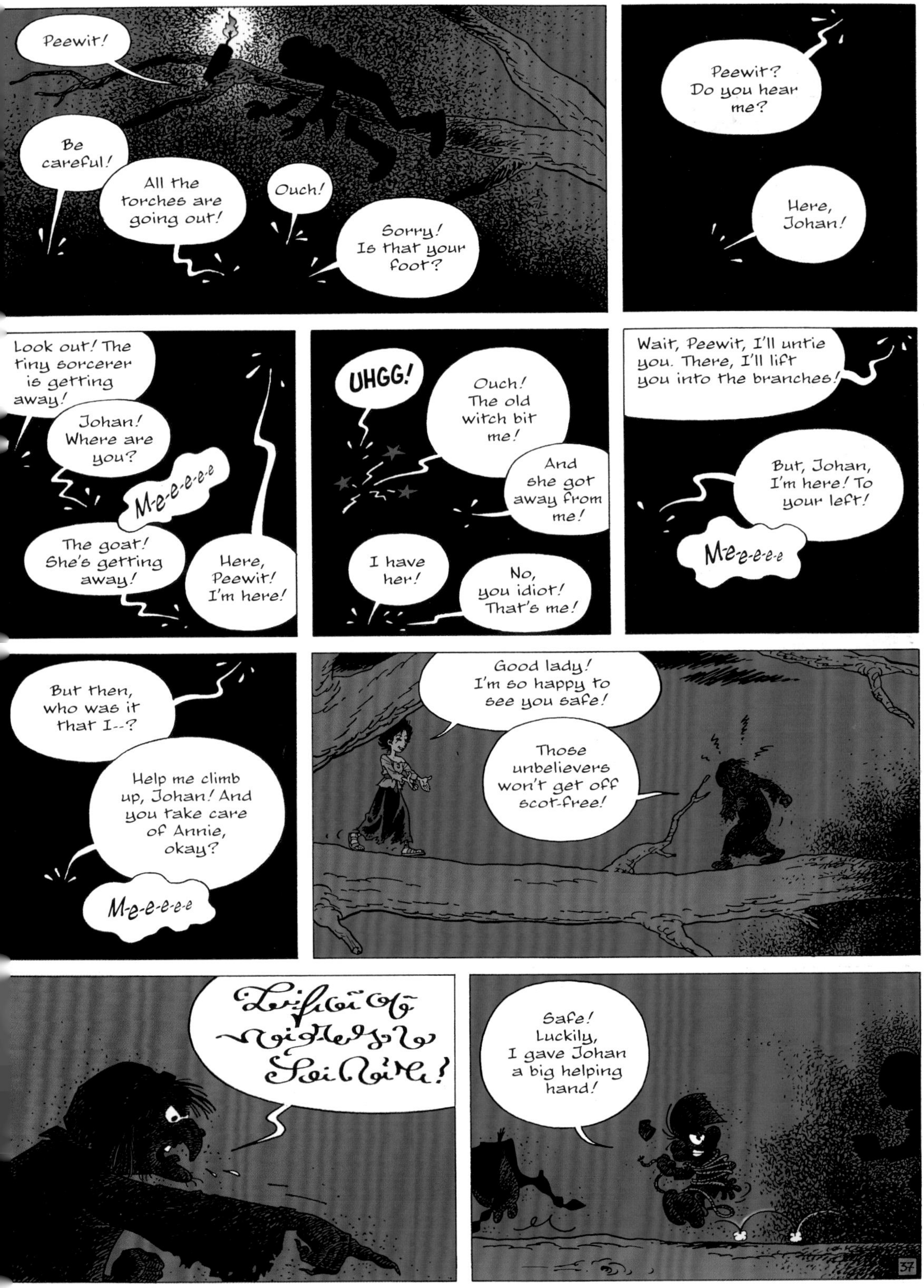
Peewit!
Be careful!
All the torches are going out!
Ouch!
Sorry! Is that your foot?
Peewit? Do you hear me?
Here, Johan!
Look out! The tiny sorcerer is getting away!
Johan! Where are you?
M-e-e-e-e-e
The goat! She's getting away!
Here, Peewit! I'm here!
UHGG!
Ouch! The old witch bit me!
And she got away from me!
I have her!
No, you idiot! That's me!
Wait, Peewit, I'll untie you. There, I'll lift you into the branches!
But, Johan, I'm here! To your left!
M-e-e-e-e-e
But then, who was it that I--?
Help me climb up, Johan! And you take care of Annie, okay?
M-e-e-e-e-e
Good lady! I'm so happy to see you safe!
Those unbelievers won't get off scot-free!
Safe! Luckily, I gave Johan a big helping hand!
37

My goodness, they've been drinking!

So, did you bring us sorcerers to burn?

HIC! They used-- HIC! A diabol-- HIC! Spell-- HIC! But they haven't-- HIC! Heard the last of m-- HIC!

Do you have the bird call, Amandine? It's getting darker.

Of course, Mom!

FWEeeettt

Luckily, there are still lots of fireflies this time of the year!

Here, Peewit, you'll light the way for us!

Will you accompany us to Bald Mountain, my dear?

No, no, go on ahead... I'm gathering some broom plant...

Ah, yes, I see why! Safe travels!

Meanwhile...

And there, good Oliver, we've taken the first step!

I don't know where you are at the moment, Miriam, but I know where to capture you!

38

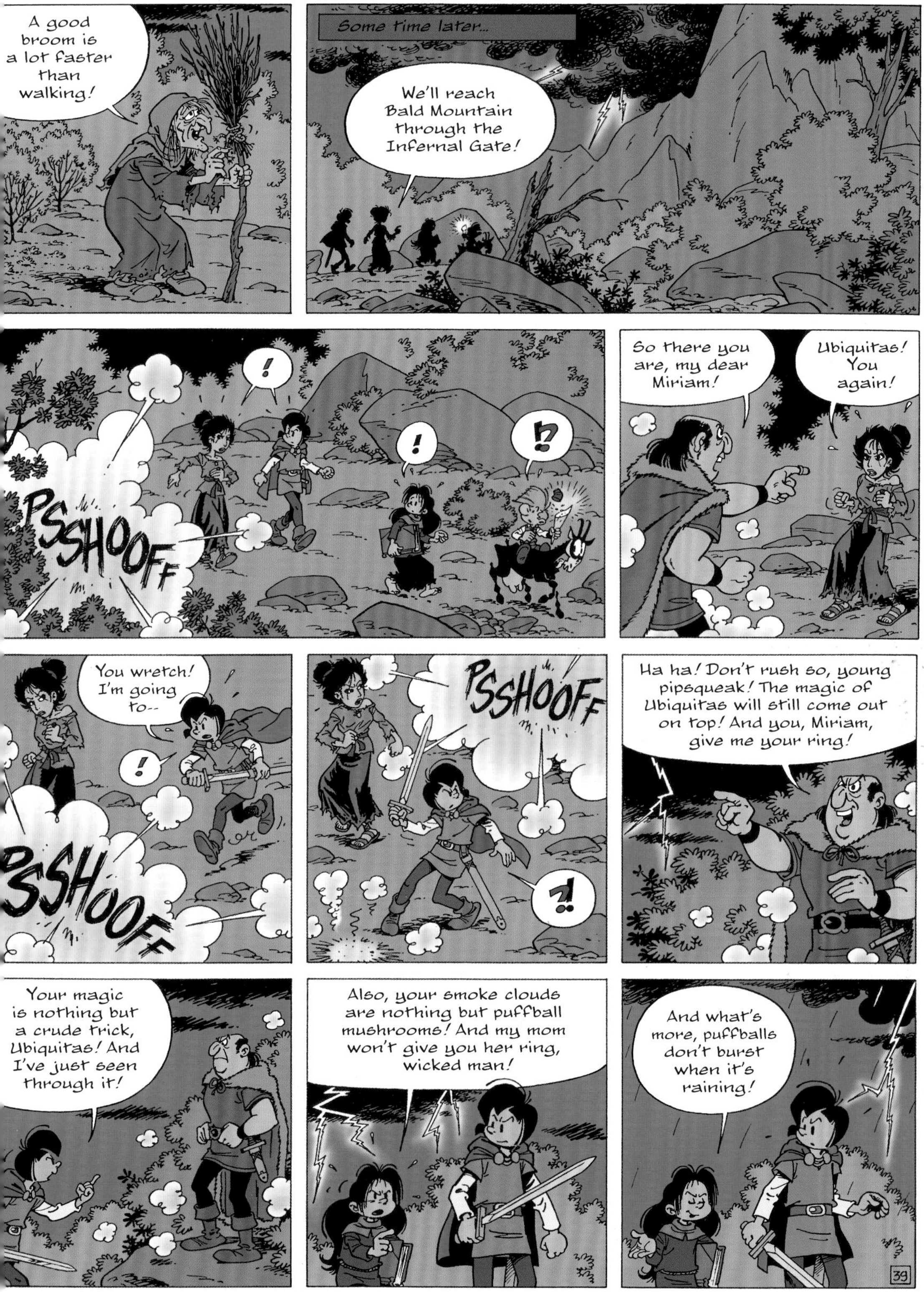
A good broom is a lot faster than walking!
Some time later...
We'll reach Bald Mountain through the Infernal Gate!
!
!
!?
PSSHOOFF
So there you are, my dear Miriam!
Ubiquitas! You again!
You wretch! I'm going to--
!
PSSHOOFF
PSSHOOFF
?!
Ha ha! Don't rush so, young pipsqueak! The magic of Ubiquitas will still come out on top! And you, Miriam, give me your ring!
Your magic is nothing but a crude trick, Ubiquitas! And I've just seen through it!
Also, your smoke clouds are nothing but puffball mushrooms! And my mom won't give you her ring, wicked man!
And what's more, puffballs don't burst when it's raining!
39

PSSHOOFF

PSSHOOFF

Out of my sight, young pipsqueak!

Get lost, you charlatan! Your tricks don't impress me!

Then, here's something to impress you!

Aaah! Pepper! My eyes!

PeeeeWlllT!

I'll teach you to hurt my friend, Johan!

Let my brother go!

There are two of them!

I noticed that! Only one is wearing a golden thimble on his finger!

?

You'll have trouble recognizing them now, Johan... Here's the thimble!

The golden thimble! Give that back to me, vermin!

Lady Miriam! Amandine! Quickly go to the ceremony on Bald Mountain! I'll hold these two crooks at bay!

40

Stay here, my good fellows! I'm quite capable of holding my own against two!

How about three?

WAP

We can still get ahold of the Globe of Power! Tie him up!

...and meanwhile...

I assure you, Oliver. This waterfall doesn't appear on the map!

At the same time, far from there...

Yes, yes, I assure you, Master Cerberus, he's the one carrying two parts of the Globe of Power.

!

May... may I come in?

41

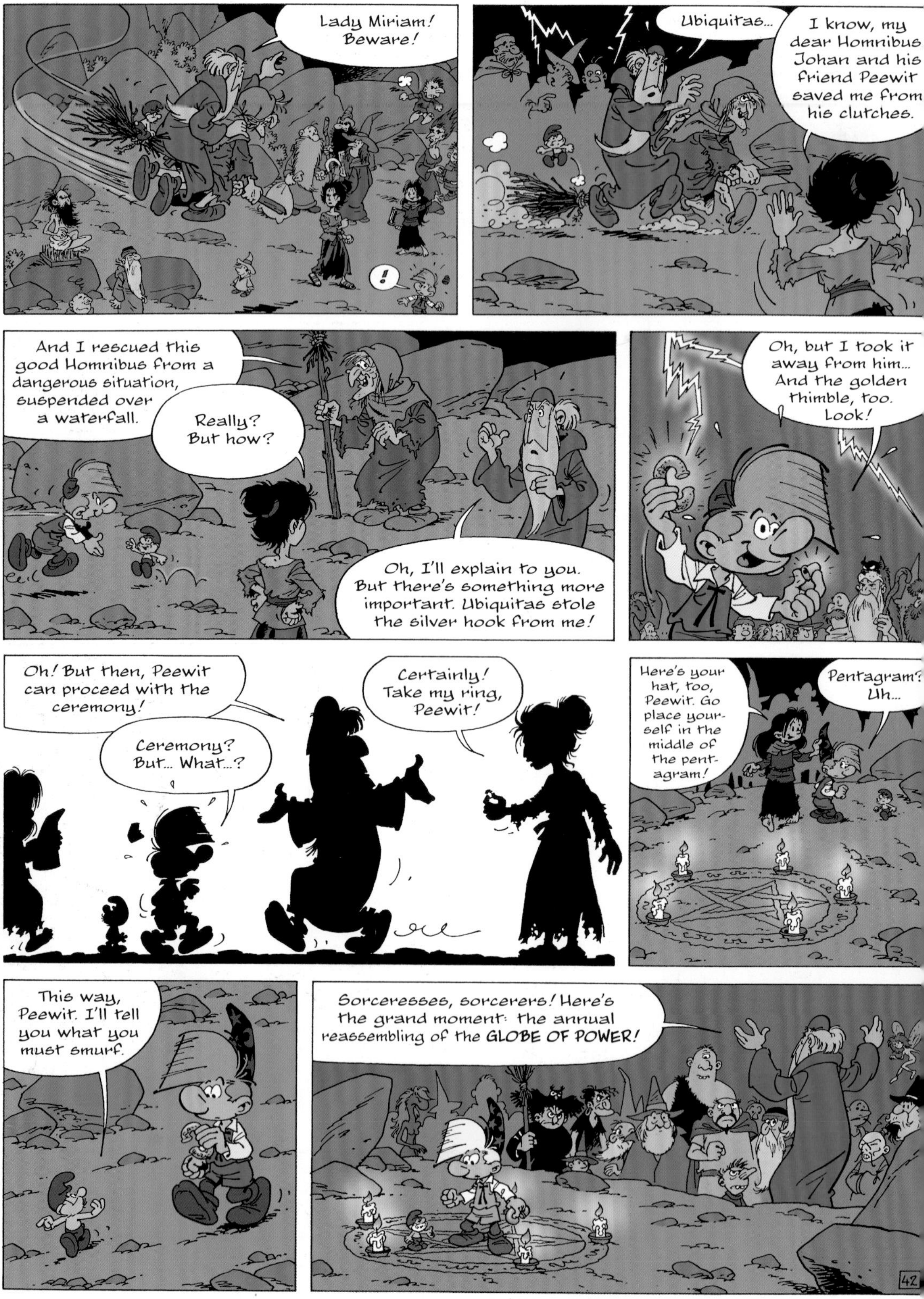

Lady Miriam! Beware!
!
Ubiquitas...
I know, my dear Homnibus. Johan and his friend Peewit saved me from his clutches.
And I rescued this good Homnibus from a dangerous situation, suspended over a waterfall.
Really? But how?
Oh, I'll explain to you. But there's something more important. Ubiquitas stole the silver hook from me!
Oh, but I took it away from him... And the golden thimble, too. Look!
Oh! But then, Peewit can proceed with the ceremony!
Ceremony? But... What...?
Certainly! Take my ring, Peewit!
Here's your hat, too, Peewit. Go place yourself in the middle of the pentagram!
Pentagram? Uh...
This way, Peewit. I'll tell you what you must smurf.
Sorceresses, sorcerers! Here's the grand moment: the annual reassembling of the GLOBE OF POWER!
42

Smurf the thimble between your thumb and index finger, and the ring in your left hand... Now, smurf the thimble in the ring...

Like that?

Now smurf the silver hook on top of the two other pieces so that the whole thing will smurf together.

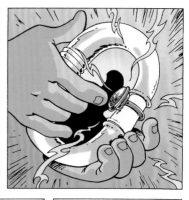

The Globe of Power has recharged its powers!

But then, with this, I'm the most powerful sorcerer in the world?

That's right, Peewit.

I can ask for anything I want? Barrels of wine, breaded, fattened chickens, musical instruments, some...

Or even better! I can have myself named king in place of the King, marry a princess, no, several princesses, rule over the whole earth, and--

No, Peewit. Inside that pentagram, you don't smurf any powers. And if you come out of the Pentagram...

...Since you're the one who put it together, you'll be struck by lightning!

Li-- lightning?!

...And here's the thunderclap!

!?

Hey! The little one! Give us what you've got there!

Yeah, or else your buddy is going to come to a bad end.

Don't listen to him, Peewit!

Those scoundrels would be capable of that!

All right! Set Johan free!

Throw us the Globe of Power first!

Here!

It's mine!

No! Mine!

Mine!

No!

Not to them!

We're doomed!

BAM

I'd better save this. Those bumblers will damage it!

NNNGNN

Here's your ring back, Mom!

44

To you, Master Homnibus, your silver hook.

...But to whom will we entrust the golden thimble?

I think Princess Loveforest is the clear choice!

A princess? There's a princess? Where?

Princess, I have the honor of entrusting this jewel with you. I know that you'll be worthy of it.

!

That, a princess? In that get-up?! No way, this is a joke!

PEEWIT!

My young friend, don't let me catch you disrespecting me again!

Uh... Princess... I didn't mean to, uh...

And what do we do with these three?

We must make an example of them!

I know!

From now on, for the rest of their existence, their magic tricks will fail lamentably!

Imposters!

Never again will they dare attack real sorcerers!

Go! Begone!

Hey there! The sun's rising, and I still have to take my test!

45

The crowing of a distant rooster marks the end of the Night of Sorcerers. The nighttime storm has dissipated, and calm has returned to the countryside and to Bald Mountain.

I PASSED! I have my sorcerer's apprentice diploma!

Ah, Johan...

How can we thank you for what you've done for us? Without you, an awful fate would have ruled over our world.

Uh... I don't know what to say!

Well, I know!

?

Peewit, you're marvelous!

SMOOOOCH

Gooo agooo...

Well, Johan, these emotions are giving me the-- HiC!...

Come, Peewit. It's time to get home to the castle.

Hic! Hic! Hic! Hic! Hic! Hic!

The End

THE SMURF FROM OUTER SPACE

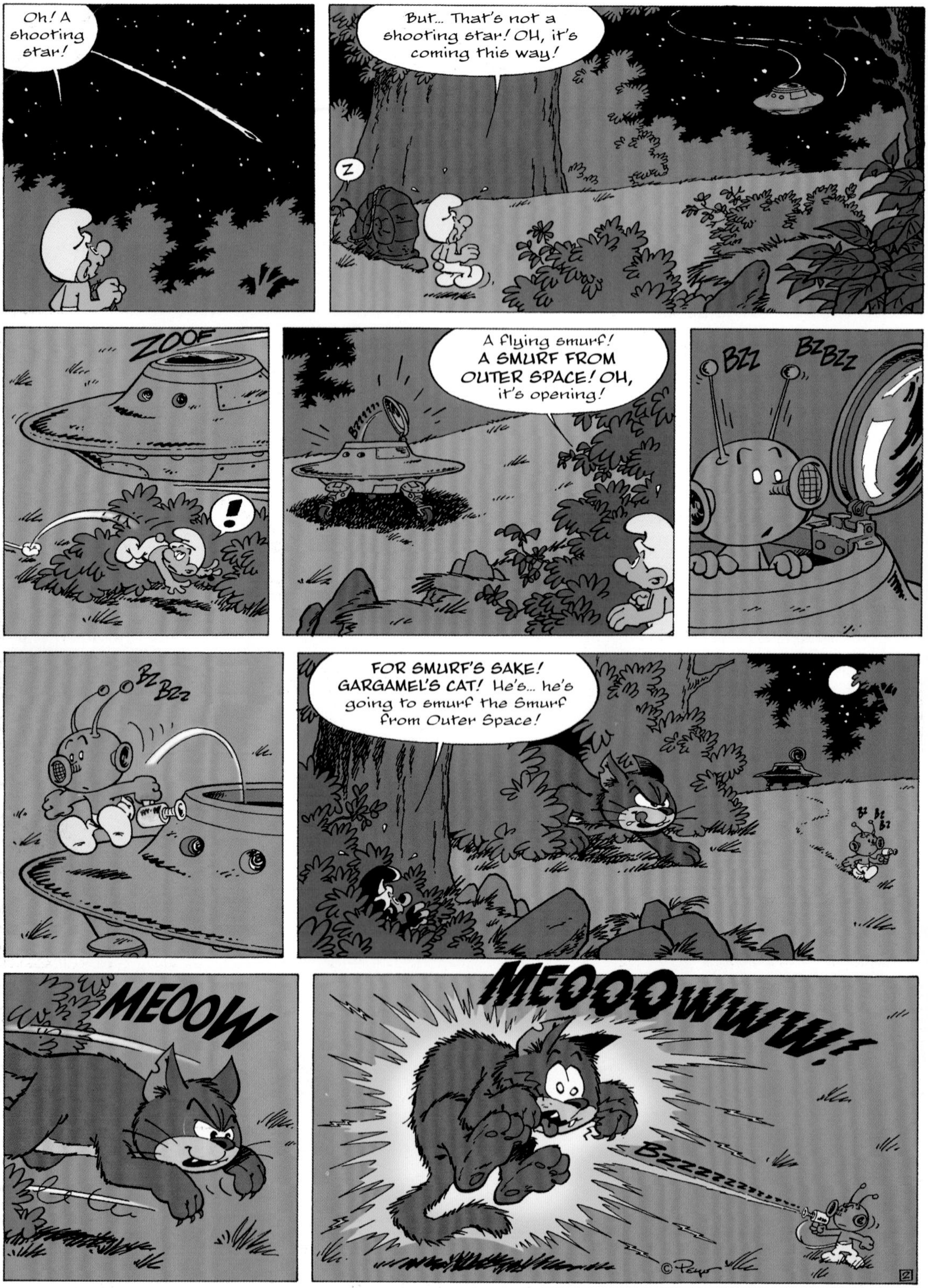
Oh! A shooting star!
But... That's not a shooting star! OH, it's coming this way!
Z
ZOOF
!
A flying smurf! A SMURF FROM OUTER SPACE! OH, it's opening!
BZZ
BZ BZZ
BZ BZZ
FOR SMURF'S SAKE! GARGAMEL'S CAT! He's... he's going to smurf the Smurf from Outer Space!
MEOOW
MEOOOWWW!!
Bzzzzzzz
©Peyo
2

MEOOOWWW MEOW MEOW

HURRAY! HURRAY!

CLAP CLAP CLAP

YIKES... He's spotted me! He's... he's going to smurf me with his green ray!

BZZ BZZZ

BZ BZZZ

BZZ... BZZ!! BRV... BRV! KRTZQLMHNL!

No... no, wait! I... I don't mean you any harm! I'm a Smurf!

BRTT!

SM.RF?!!¿ WH.TS . SM.RF?

Come with me. I have to introduce you to Papa Smurf! What's your name?

BRTT!

He doesn't look mean!

The problem is that we're far from the village! We'll have to smurf for a long time, and that's tiring...

YAWN!

KRTZ?

ZZZ...

PWWAAAT

!

YOOHOO... LAZY SMURF... WHERE ARE YOU?

BZ¿

?

That's for me! Smurfing for me...

YOOHOO! WHERE ARE YOU?

You should've told me sooner he didn't come home!

But I'd told him I'd tell you! He must still be smurfing in a bush with his snail!

YOOHOO... LAZY SMURF! YOOHOO!

101

OVER HERE!
I FOUND HIM!

What's that green Smurf?

Oh, it's a green Smurf!

Who's that?

Let me introduce BRTT! He's a Smurf from outer space! He landed in the forest with a flying smurf!

A flying smurf? I'd love to see that!

Hold on, Handy Smurf, let's see who we're dealing with first!

I'm Papa Smurf! What planet do you come from?

P.P. SM.RF¿ BRTT! H.LL.! .M FR.M TH. PL.N.T V.N.S! BL... BL!...!

PWAT
PWAT
PWAT

I didn't under-stand everything, but welcome, BRTT!

BRTT! BRTT!

He's cute!

Here, BRTT, I have a gift for you!

G.FT¿

Yes, for you! Go ahead, open it! Hee hee!

BROOF

H.! H.! H.! H.! G.FT... BR..F! BR..F! BR..F! H.! H.! H.!

It makes him smurf! He's funny! Hee hee hee!

G.FT! FRY, G.FT!

A gift for me? That's nice!

H.! H.! H.! F.NNY! H.! H.! H.!

Bzzzzz...

© Peyo

4

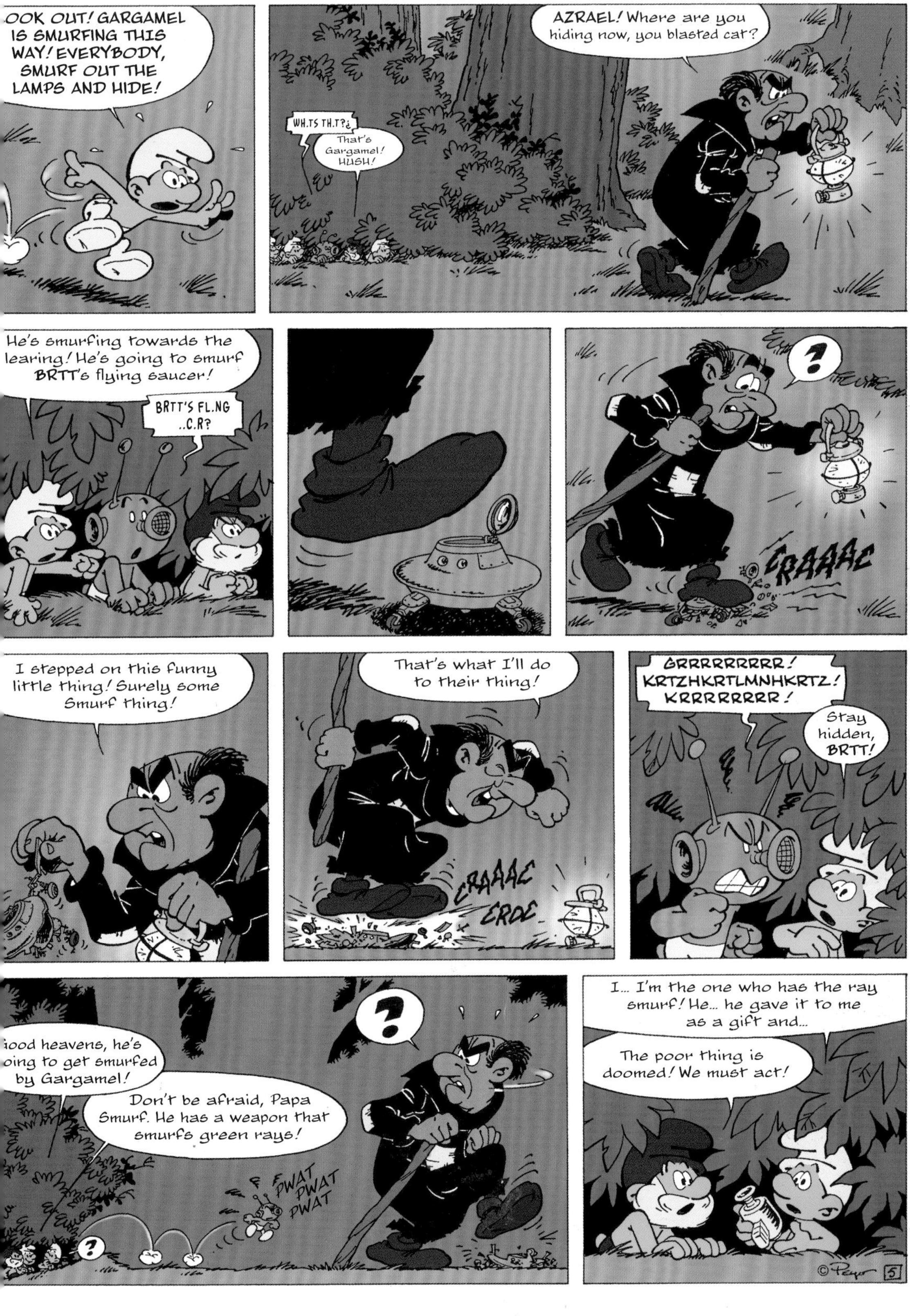

OOK OUT! GARGAMEL IS SMURFING THIS WAY! EVERYBODY, SMURF OUT THE LAMPS AND HIDE!
WH.TS TH.T?¿
That's Gargamel! HUSH!
AZRAEL! Where are you hiding now, you blasted cat?
He's smurfing towards the learing! He's going to smurf BRTT's flying saucer!
BRTT'S FL.NG ..C.R?
?
CRAAAC
I stepped on this funny little thing! Surely some Smurf thing!
That's what I'll do to their thing!
CRAAAC
CROC
GRRRRRRRRR! KRTZHKRTLMNHKRTZ! KRRRRRRRR!
Stay hidden, BRTT!
?
iood heavens, he's oing to get smurfed by Gargamel!
Don't be afraid, Papa Smurf. He has a weapon that smurfs green rays!
PWAT PWAT PWAT
?
I... I'm the one who has the ray smurf! He... he gave it to me as a gift and...
The poor thing is doomed! We must act!
© Peyo
5

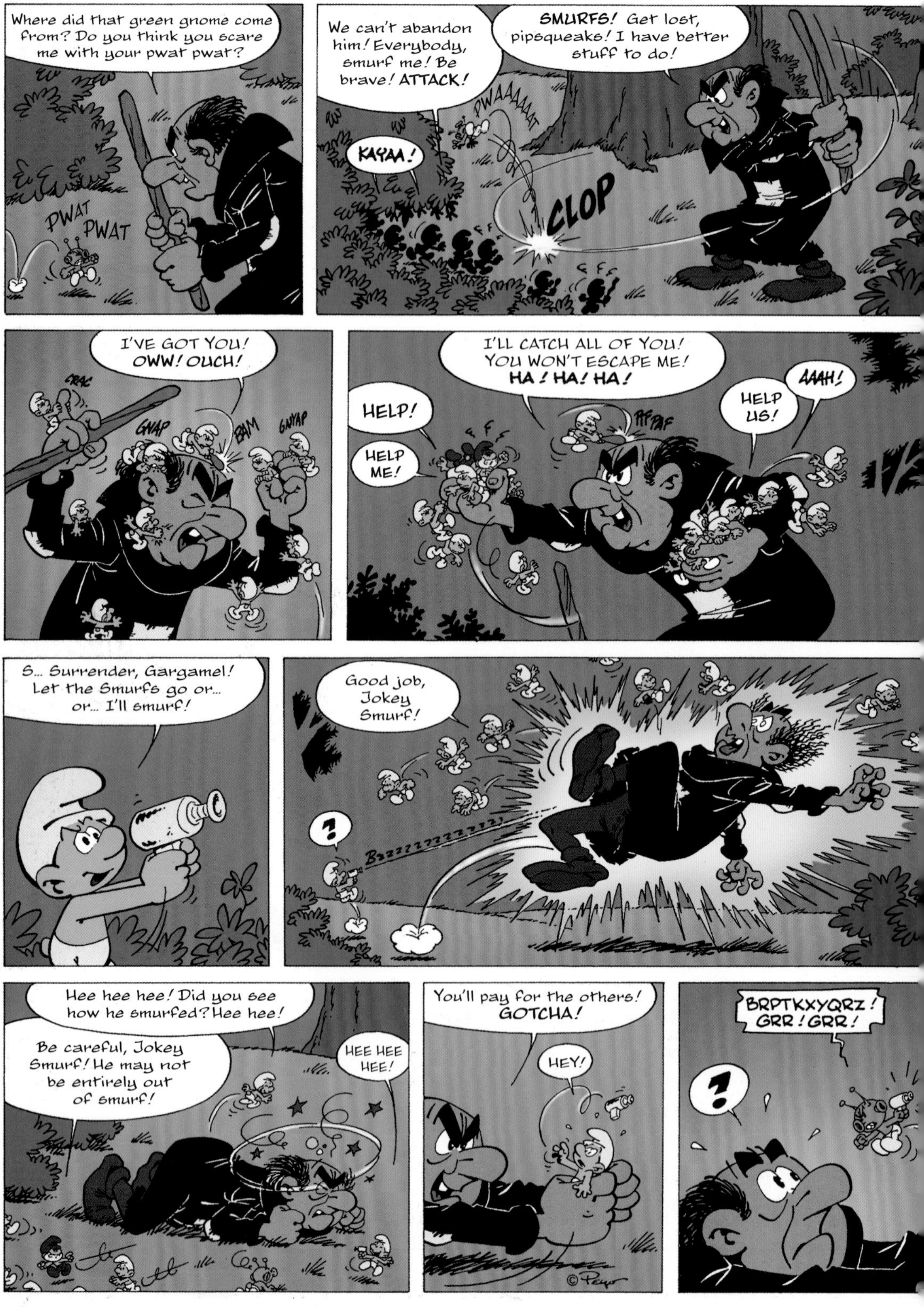
Where did that green gnome come from? Do you think you scare me with your pwat pwat?
PWAT PWAT
We can't abandon him! Everybody, smurf me! Be brave! ATTACK!
KAYAA!
PWAAAAAAT
SMURFS! Get lost, pipsqueaks! I have better stuff to do!
CLOP
I'VE GOT YOU! OWW! OUCH!
CRAC
GNAP
BAM
GNYAP
I'LL CATCH ALL OF YOU! YOU WON'T ESCAPE ME! HA! HA! HA!
HELP!
HELP ME!
HELP US!
AAAH!
S... Surrender, Gargamel! Let the Smurfs go or... or... I'll smurf!
Good job, Jokey Smurf!
?
Hee hee hee! Did you see how he smurfed? Hee hee!
Be careful, Jokey Smurf! He may not be entirely out of smurf!
HEE HEE HEE!
You'll pay for the others! GOTCHA!
HEY!
© Peyo
BRPTKXYQRZ! GRR! GRR!
?

GLUB!

KRRTZ!

Good job! Hee hee!

AAAAAH! OWW! OUCH! That's hot!

Bmm

BRTTPRT!

Hee hee!

Ha ha ha!

Hurray, BRTT!

Hee hee hee!

BRPP! BR.K.N!

Come with us. We're returning to the village! I'll smurf what I can for your smurf!

A little later...

Do you want a gift, BRTT?

Do you want a cake?

He's sad. Nothing makes him happy. Not even my book of sayings!

Hmm...!

Do you want a nice sarsaparilla smurf?

BRTT, W.NT T. G. H.M.!

What's he saying?

I think he'd really like to go home... But how?

The next morning...

Go tell Papa Smurf that Blacksmith Smurf and I have a surprise for BRTT!

Right away, Handy Smurf!

BING BING

Oh, is that right? BRTT, come see. We have a surprise for you!

P... S..., Handy Smurf........! — .... ?

S.RPR.S.? F.R M.?

©Peyo

7

105

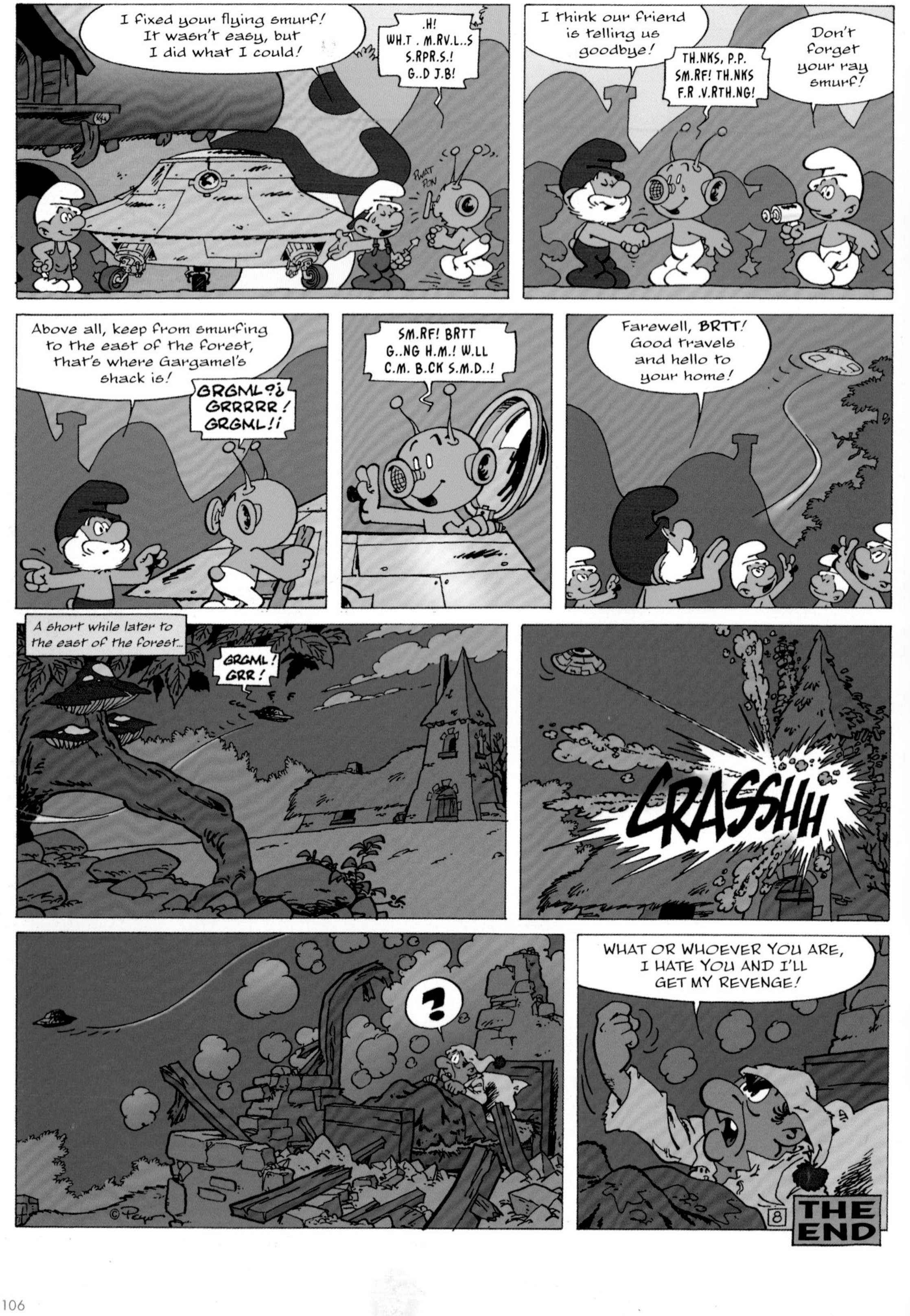
I fixed your flying smurf! It wasn't easy, but I did what I could!
.H! WH.T . M.RV.L..S S.RPR.S.! G..D J.B!
I think our friend is telling us goodbye!
TH.NKS, P.P. SM.RF! TH.NKS F.R .V.RTH.NG!
Don't forget your ray smurf!
Above all, keep from smurfing to the east of the forest, that's where Gargamel's shack is!
GRGML?¿ GRRRRR! GRGML!¡
SM.RF! BRTT G..NG H.M.! W.LL C.M. B.CK S.M.D..!
Farewell, BRTT! Good travels and hello to your home!
A short while later to the east of the forest...
GRGML! GRR!
CRASSHH
?
©Peyo
WHAT OR WHOEVER YOU ARE, I HATE YOU AND I'LL GET MY REVENGE!
8
THE END

THE SMURF GAGS

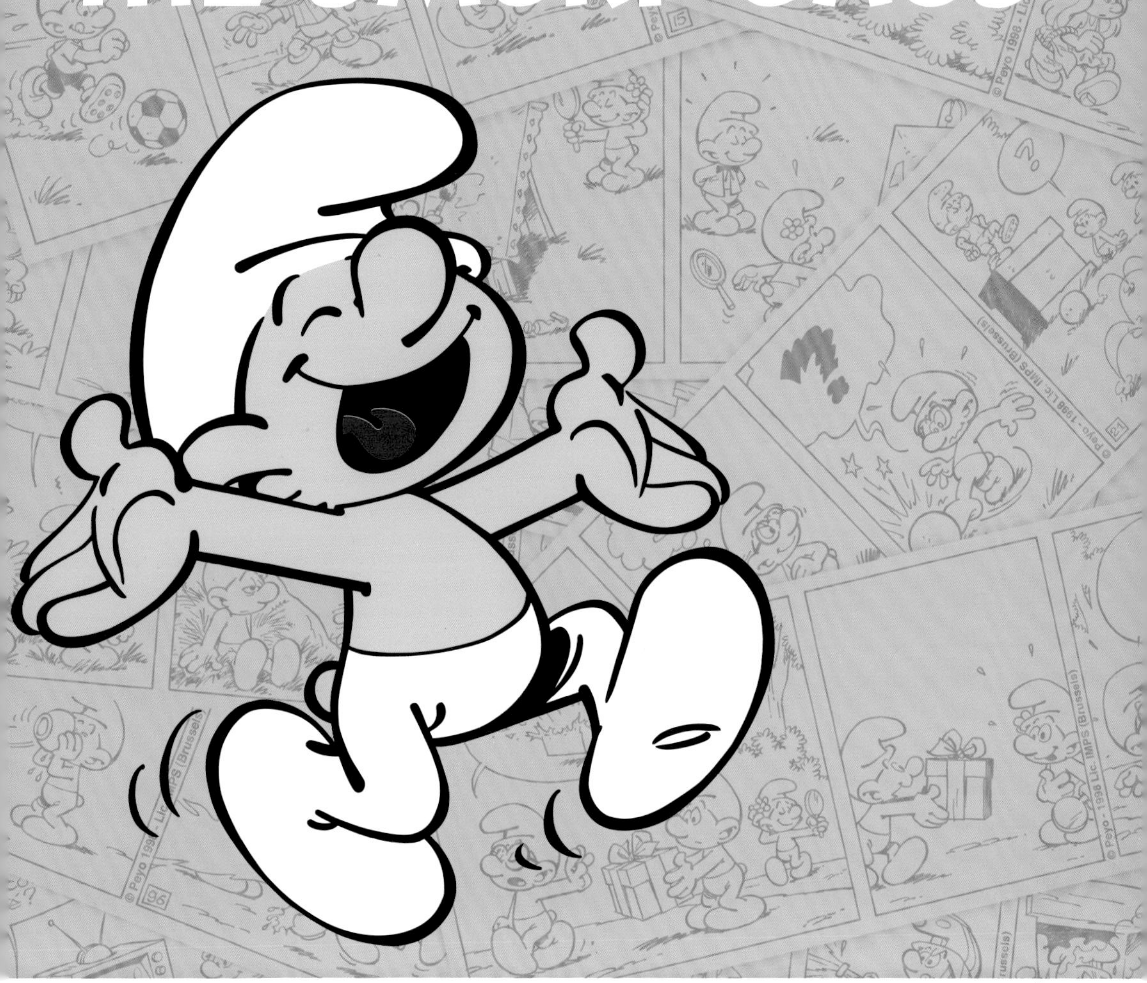

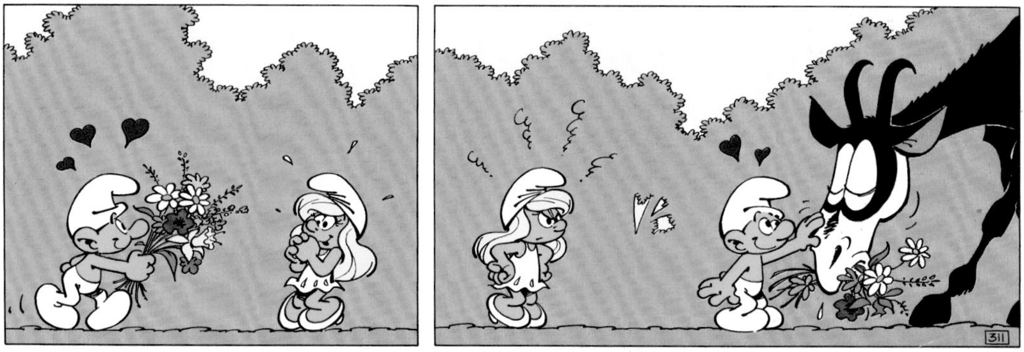
311

120 SMURF JOKES

Papa Smurf! Somebody wrote on my door that "Brainy Smurf is a pain-in-the-smurf!"

Oh! Who could have smurfed that?

Several witnesses saw him from a distance.

And I was able to smurf this police sketch.

© Peyo - 1998 Lic. IMPS (Brussels)

187

Oops! Sorry, Brainy Smurf... I think I went a little overboard on the amount of powder.

© Peyo

Hey, Dopey Smurf, there's no point in watering. It's going to smurf soon.

Well, that's why I'm hurrying to get it done beforehand.

?!

© Peyo - 2001 Lic. IMPS (Brussels)

444

109

ZING

A chocolate bar if you smurf the answer.

$4 \times 2 =$

$4 \times 2 = 2 \times 4$

That kid will go far.

Chomp Yum

Crunch Yum Gulp Chomp

Hey, Smurf, would you help me carry a beam?

It's just that... my back is hurting. I'm afraid it'll be too heavy.

Hey, I'd like to move my garden bench. Be a sweetie--

Mmyeah... It's all relative!

Hmm... You've caught Smurf measles.

Is it contagious, Papa Smurf?

545

A bit.

© Peyo - 2002 Lic. IMPS (Brussels)

You could wait, Greedy Smurf!

But this way, the carrot will be lighter.

Yes, but you'll be heavier!

168

© Peyo - 1998 Lic. IMPS (Brussels)

Would you mind holding these balloons for me for a moment?

Sure, Hefty Smurf. But why are you walking around with that dumbbell?

Oh, yeah, you're right. Why did I bring it with me?

There was a reason, though...

305

© Peyo - 2000 Lic. IMPS (Brussels)

111

Chef Smurf isn't here. Let's take advantage. Yum.

That cake was smurfly good! But I couldn't smurf the tiniest bit more! ≥Whew!≤

Greedy Smurf, I made a cake especially for you, but someone smurfed it. So, I made you another one! Dig in!

© Peyo - 1998 Lic. IMPS (Brussels)

20

Look closely, my young Smurfs! The culmination of ten years of research.

Glug Glug Glug

TADA!

? ? ?

263

No, thanks! We don't feel like rebuilding the whole village.

© Peyo - 1998 Lic. IMPS (Brussels)

Oh, look! Hefty Smurf forgot one of his dumbbells.

Come now, don't smurf that face! Taking it back to him is the least we can do, isn't it?

© Peyo - 2000 Lic. IMPS (Brussels)

329

Tell me what you think of this redcurrant juice, but don't forget to shake the jar.

!

BEFORE you open it, Dopey Smurf!

© Peyo - 2001 Lic. IMPS (Brussels)

I've always wondered why we smurf our doors since there aren't any thieves.

Well, Locksmith Smurf wouldn't have anything to do otherwise.

That's true.

© Peyo - 1998 Lic. IMPS (Brussels)

You're incorrigible, Jokey Smurf!

?

© Peyo

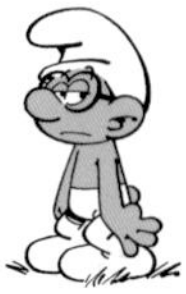

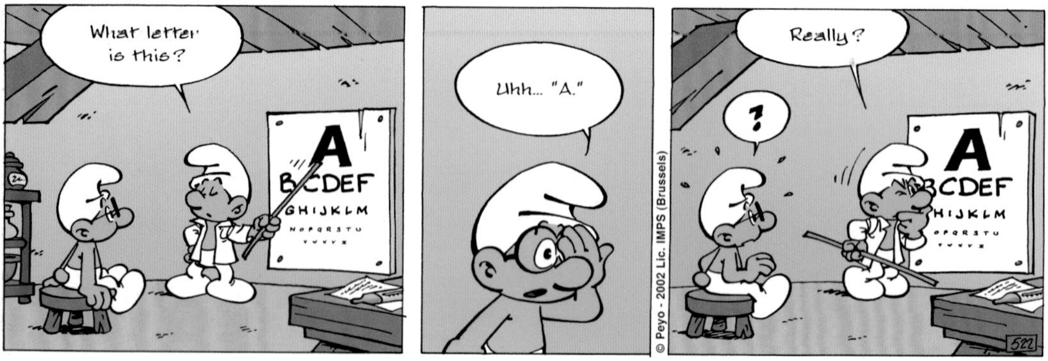
What letter is this?
A
BCDEF
GHIJKLM
Uhh... "A."
© Peyo - 2002 Lic. IMPS (Brussels)
?
Really?
A
BCDEF
HIJKLM
522

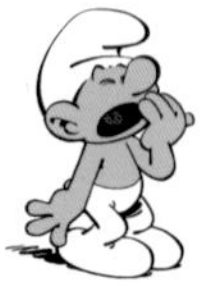

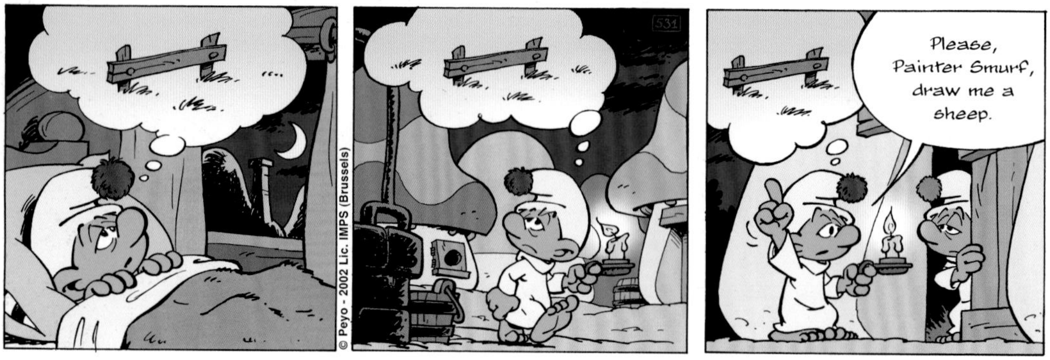
© Peyo - 2002 Lic. IMPS (Brussels)
531
Please, Painter Smurf, draw me a sheep.

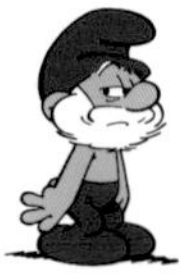

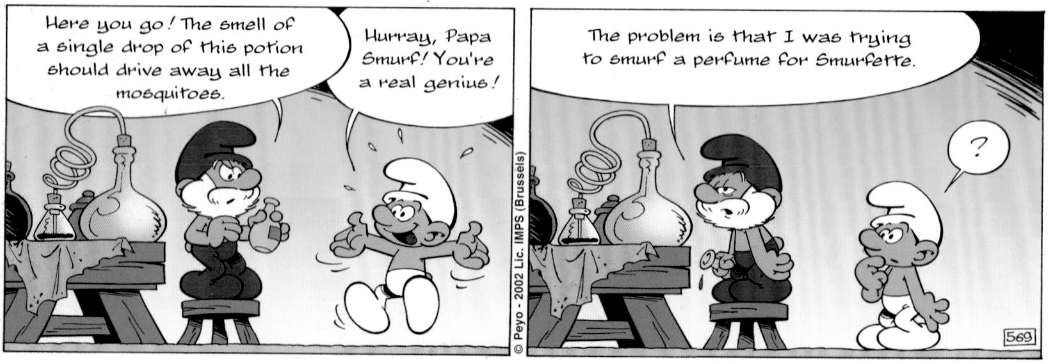
Here you go! The smell of a single drop of this potion should drive away all the mosquitoes.
Hurray, Papa Smurf! You're a real genius!
© Peyo - 2002 Lic. IMPS (Brussels)
The problem is that I was trying to smurf a perfume for Smurfette.
?
569

Handy Smurf, look out! The strikers are smurfing towards you!

Let him try and smurf that one!

380

?!

KCK

What?! -11 F?

It's so cold, I brought the thermometer in.

That's very kind, Dopey Smurf...

347

© Peyo - 2000 Lic. IMPS (Brussels)

You changed out the frame for your window. Is that a good model?

SHLAK

YEOOW

VERY good!

374

Honestly, Clumsy Smurf, you should give up on that idea of a record for length of time on a swing.

© Peyo - 1998 Lic. IMPS (Brussels)

What a heatwave! It's so hot, I'm afraid of smurfing in my house.

I smurfed myself a fan.

That looks great! How does it smurf?

Oh, it's as simple as smurf.

© Peyo - 1998 Lic. IMPS (Brussels)

You just... ≷hff≷... have to... ≷pff≷... pedal! ≷hff!≷

I'm going to smurf you to sleep with a song, Baby.

Arooo!

Rock-a-smurf baby, in a smurf top...

What?! You're not sleeping yet?

Beleb!

© Peyo - 1998 Lic. IMPS (Brussels)

© Peyo - 1998 Lic. IMPS (Brussels)

Here's a gift for you, Brainy Smurf.

Oh, no! But thanks a lot, Jokey Smurf.

Here's a gift for--

No, no! Ha ha! Good ol' Jokey Smurf!

But what's gotten into all of them lately?

SNIF

© Peyo - 1998 Lic. IMPS (Brussels)

© Peyo - 1998 Lic. IMPS (Brussels)

316

Lazy Smurf! You could get down and help us!

Someone has to guide you.

© Peyo - 2000 Lic. IMPS (Brussels)

332

Where's that do-nothing Lazy Smurf gone off to now?

?

I'm on my way, Lazy Sm...

336

© Peyo - 2000 Lic. IMPS (Brussels)

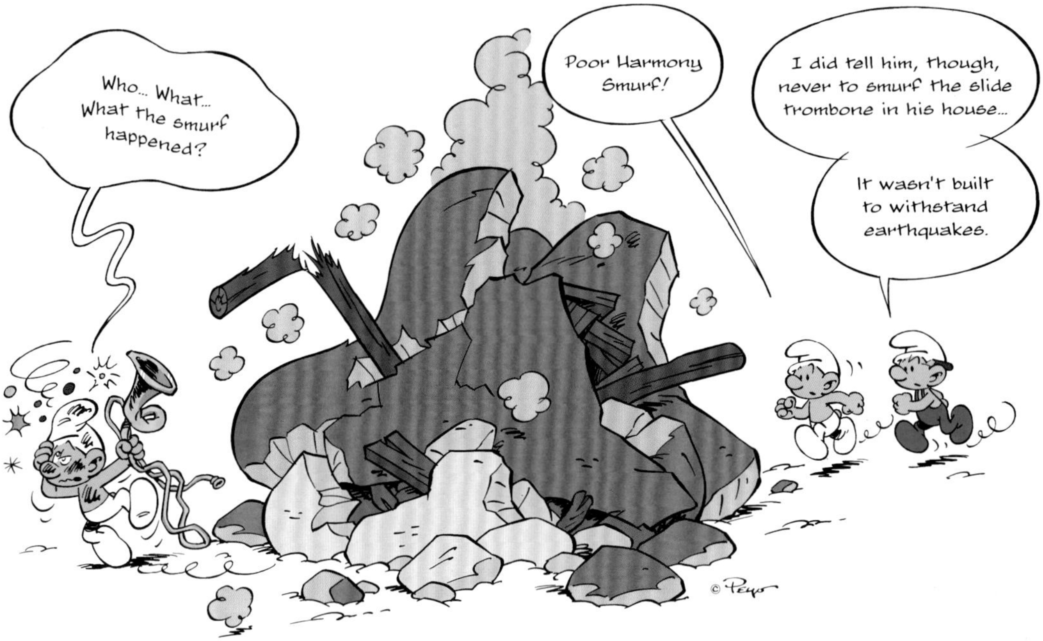
Who... What...
What the smurf happened?
Poor Harmony Smurf!
I did tell him, though, never to smurf the slide trombone in his house...
It wasn't built to withstand earthquakes.
© Peyo

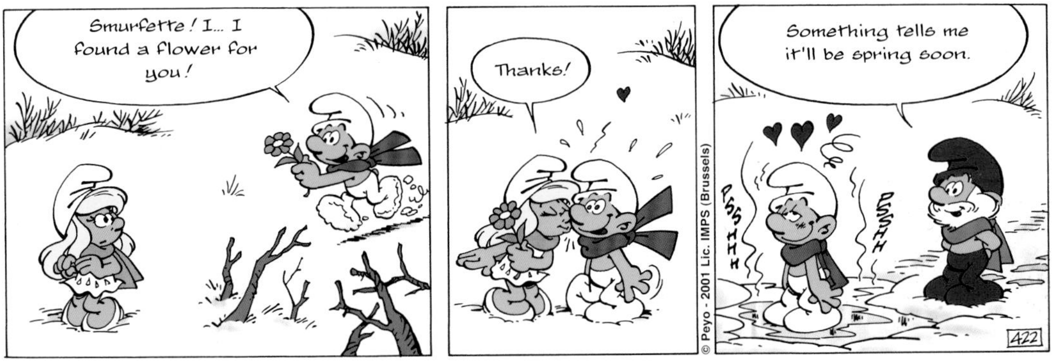
Smurfette! I... I found a flower for you!
Thanks!
© Peyo - 2001 Lic. IMPS (Brussels)
Something tells me it'll be spring soon.
PSSHHH
PSSHHH
422

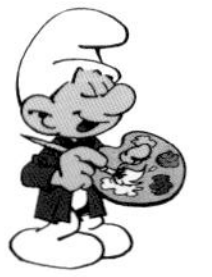

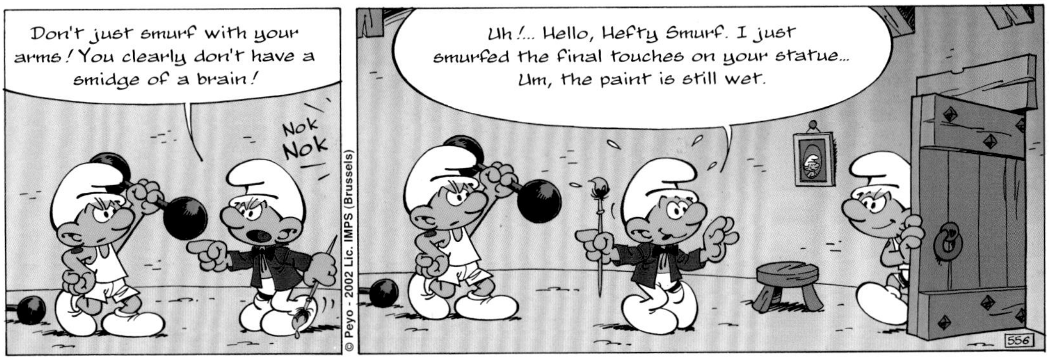
Don't just smurf with your arms! You clearly don't have a smidge of a brain!
Nok Nok
© Peyo - 2002 Lic. IMPS (Brussels)
Uh!... Hello, Hefty Smurf. I just smurfed the final touches on your statue... Um, the paint is still wet.
556

Oh! You're smurfing my ears! Here, have a sucker!

‡WAAH!‡

Come on, Smurfette, you can't give him a sucker every time he smurfs! That's anti-educational. You're going to smurf him bad habits, and as Papa Smurf always says--

...

© Peyo - 2003 Lic. IMPS (Brussels)

612

I'm going to smurf a song to the sun!

I swear to you, I didn't know it smurfed!

© Peyo - 2003 Lic. IMPS (Brussels)

639

Well, Hefty Smurf! What are you smurfing?

Heh heh! I'm training for the next Olympics.

© Peyo - 2002 Lic. IMPS (Brussels)

5-77

Abracadabra... And hup!

And now Clumsy Smurf is going to smurf up next as... uh... a knife thrower!

© Peyo - 2003 Lic. IMPS (Brussels)

I'm sure that a few days of hiking with his gear on his back will smurf him character.

Lazy Smurf, are you ready?

Yes, yes, let's go!

What's up?

© Peyo - 2003 Lic. IMPS (Brussels)

6-10

Papa Smurf, we have something to ask you.

Yes?

Well, here goes... We... Uh, that's to say... So...

Poor Timid Smurf! He just can't say it.

Then you say it, Distracted Smurf.

Me?! Uh... I've forgotten what it was.

607

Exotic Cuisine

053

Did Smurfette tell you to meet her here at noon, too, Distracted Smurf?

?

Smurfette?... Ah! Uh... No, she sent me to tell you she preferred to smurf you near the big oak.

585

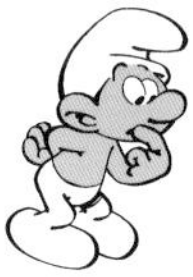

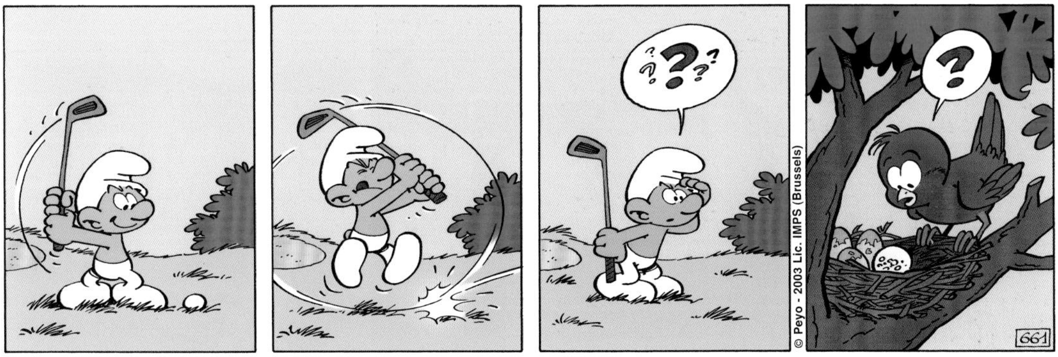

?? ? ?
?
© Peyo - 2003 Lic. IMPS (Brussels)
661

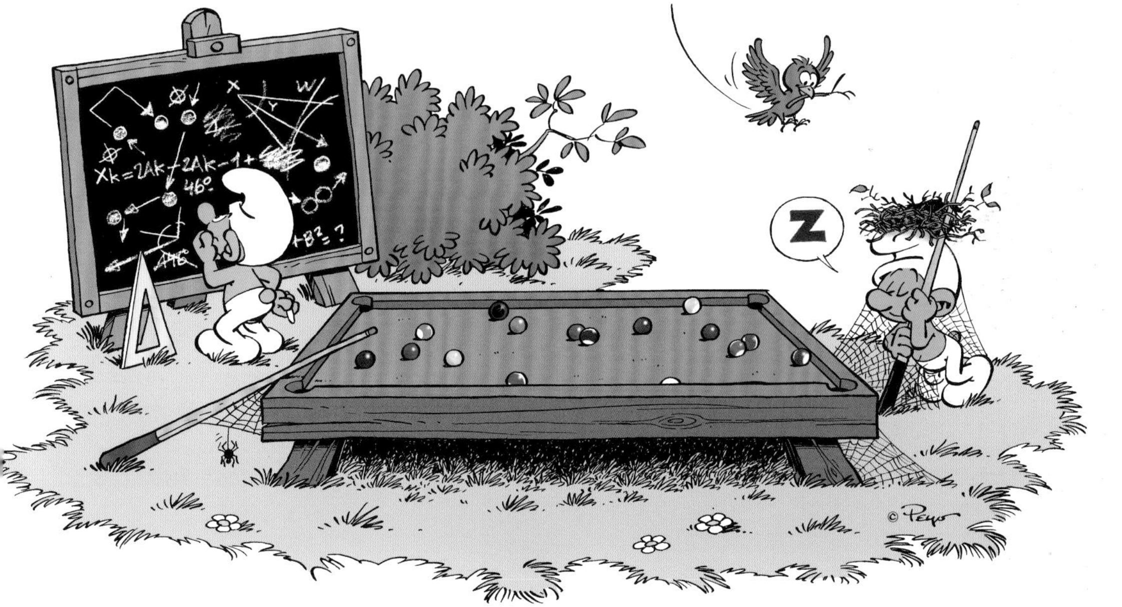

Z
© Peyo

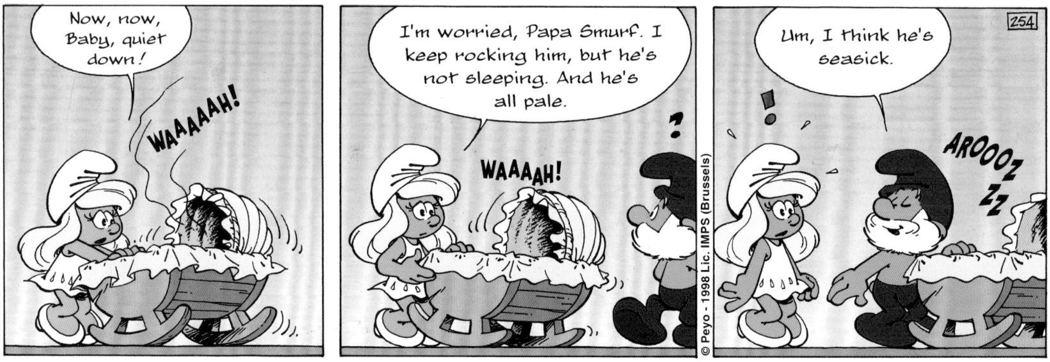

Now, now, Baby, quiet down!
WAAAAAH!
I'm worried, Papa Smurf. I keep rocking him, but he's not sleeping. And he's all pale.
WAAAAH!
?
© Peyo - 1998 Lic. IMPS (Brussels)
254
!
Um, I think he's seasick.
AROOOZ
ZZ

The important thing in work is being organized and looking ahead. You must smurf good PLANNING.

I'll write it on the board. PL-AN-NI...

NG... Uh...

665

♪

Oh, hello, Smurfette! Careful, I could've doused you!

679

You know, Papa Smurf, sometimes I think I have a curse hanging over me.

Come, come, Unlucky Smurf. You know full well that's nothing but superstition.

Some things are simply, how do I put it... uh... smurfly difficult... uh... to explain!

499

Greedy Smurf, you're the only one who prefers my still lifes.

474

433

Well? Do you see the dragon from atop that rock?

Nothing on the horizon!

?

The coward! He's afraid of me, that's for sure!

364

Lazy Smurf, just when will you finish smurfing your wall?

Uh... I'm working on it, Papa Smurf!

Oh, yeah?

344

© Peyo - 2000 Lic. IMPS (Brussels)

?!

298

© Peyo - 1998 Lic. IMPS (Brussels)

"...I'm in love with Smurfette..."

This way, the whole sky will know!

The whole pond, too!

I ♥ Smurfette

¿Gulp!¿ Now I just have to let Smurfette know!

© Peyo - 1998 Lic. IMPS (Brussels)

...But, as it's smurfed in the Memoirs of Brainy Smurf... Blabla... Blabla... Bla...

So, I smurfed him straight in the eyes: "Who smurfs a smurf... and so on and so forth..." Obviously, he remained smurfed in his spot!

Aaah! Getting to talk without being interrupted does me good!

© Peyo - 1998 Lic. IMPS (Brussels)

127

Dopey Smurf! How can you be so smurf? If you turned your wheelbarrow over, it would roll!

Yes... But then, someone would make me work.

Look, Papa Smurf, I made a curling iron for Smurfette!

Excellent idea, Handy Smurf, but you'd better smurf some test runs!

Come on, be nice, Papa Smurf! It's for Smurfette!

At these words, the crow opens its beak, ..., ..., and drops its smurf!

?

...AND DROPS ITS SMURF, Greedy Smurf!

Oh, my! This really is no time to go for a walk!

Smurfnabbit! This really is no time to be working!

What? You think this gift is going to blow up in your face? Oh, come on now, what do you smurf by that?!

Times really have changed... This truly is a gift!

¿PFF...!¿ This is no good. I can't even manage to convince myself.

What?! Handy Smurf is resting... Let's let him sleep. He works so hard.

Hello, Papa Smurf!

!?

LAZY SMURF!

529

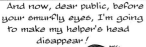

And now, dear public, before your smurfly eyes, I'm going to make my helper's head disappear!

Meh! We've seen that!

Yeah! We know that trick! ⋮YAWN!⋮

?

⋮Hmm!⋮ I wonder if I should completely resmurf that trick.

?

© Peyo - 2000 Lic. IMPS (Brussels)

385

173

© Peyo - 1998 Lic. IMPS (Brussels)

Hello, Harmony Smurf! I've come to tune your piano.

But... I didn't ask you to.

You didn't, but your neighbor did.

?

© Peyo - 2001 Lic. IMPS (Brussels)

456

Here's your hellebore leaf, Papa Smurf!
Well, you sure took your time!
Ouch?! But this isn't hellebore! It's stinging nettle!
484
© Peyo - 2002 Lic. IMPS (Brussels)
Really?!
Uh... It's all right now! Thanks anyway, Dopey Smurf!

Hey! I've got a bite!
WOW! That's probably the biggest thing I've ever smurfed!
But it's just an old
© Peyo - 2001 Lic. IMPS (Brussels)
Yes, but it's at least a size 13!
?
452

Hi, Grouchy Smurf! Nasty weather, isn't it? It's smurfly cold!
!
Well, winter's on the way... Me, I don't like winter!
© Peyo - 1998 Lic. IMPS (Brussels)
AND ME?! I DON'T LIKE ANYONE STEALING MY LINES!
175

I smurf a little of Papa Smurf's growth hormones on this mushroom, and...

ZOOF

Apartments to smurf

60

For real? I can help you?

Of course, Clumsy Smurf! Here, smurf this board and go paint it outside!

This way, at least, he'll smurf me in peace and won't risk messing up my house!

I didn't smurf too bad of a job, did I?

641

Are you ready, Smurfette?

Yes, I was waiting for you.

What magnificent weather for a picnic. A clear blue sky with one little cloud!

© Peyo - 2003 Lic. IMPS (Brussels)

648

© Peyo - 2000 Lic. IMPS (Brussels)

323

© Peyo

We're smurfing an igloo, Papa Smurf!

What a good idea!

There... Typically Inuit!

© Peyo - 1998 Lic. IMPS (Brussels)

270

Please, after you.

!

Thanks, Brainy Smurf, that's very kind!

Don't mention it!

576

© Peyo - 2002 Lic. IMPS (Brussels)

Baby Smurf wants a story before going to sleep.

AGAIN?

Honestly, I think we spoil him a little too much!

Arhoo! Arhoo!

© Peyo - 1998 Lic. IMPS (Brussels)

249

Me, I don't like the sun! I don't like the heat and I don't like Smurfs laughing!

What's that grump smurfing about now?

He says the sky is blue, that it's going to be nice and hot, and that everyone will be happy!

Lazy Smurf, how can you sleep all the time like that? Isn't there a dream that you'd like to accomplish?

No...

Ah, yes! I'd like to become Papa Smurf!

Fine... Keep dreaming!

Ah! I'll be good smurfing my new concerto here.

Here's your bow, Harmony Smurf!

Oh, no! He's going to smurf our ears again!

DZING
DZOiiiNG

But... this isn't my bow, it's a metal saw!

I'm sorry! It's crazy how distracted I can get!

No more smurfing, you filthy things... Flyswatter the Terrible is here!

ZWIP ZWIP ZWIP ZWIP

Bzz Bzz Bzz

© Peyo - 1998 Lic. IMPS (Brussels)

274

GRAND SMURFED BALL
Jurassic Smurf

HUP! HUP!

© Peyo - 2002 Lic. IMPS (Brussels)

Here are your glasses back, Brainy Smurf.

Thanks, Hefty Smurf! Ever since you've been training with my glasses on, Smurfette's crazy about me, and nobody's smurfing me on the head with mallets!

565

How about that diet, Smurfette?

Oh, I haven't lost a single ounce! And yours?

Me either! I don't get it!

Honestly, it's smurfed my morale in the pits!

Let's go have some ice cream to comfort ourselves!

Good idea!

© Peyo - 2003 Lic. IMPS (Brussels)

650

My goodness! That's the first time I've ever seen anyone that attached to Brainy Smurf!

Me too, and it's a pleasure to see!

They look smurfly close!

You can say that again!

© Peyo - 2001 Lic. IMPS (Brussels)

497

Hello, Smurfette? Do you remember that you promised me a kiss?

Listen closely, I'll smurf it to you... SMACK!

≥PFF,≤ before the invention of the telesmurf, she'd have smurfed me a real kiss!

© Peyo - 2001 Lic. IMPS (Brussels)

468

138

Painter Smurf, I'd like for you to smurf a very lifelike portrait of me, if possible!

Okay! We'll smurf it this afternoon!

Yes, but hey, I want something attractive!

Make up your mind! Lifelike or attractive?

© Peyo - 1998 Lic. IMPS (Brussels)

JOKEY SMURF! COME HERE RIGHT NOW!

© Peyo - 2002 Lic. IMPS (Brussels)

What?! That's Lazy Smurf! What could have him smurfing so fast?

© Peyo - 2003 Lic. IMPS (Brussels)

≷Whew!≷ I nearly smurfed home late for my nap!

139

IS SMURFETTE GOING TO CHANGE HER HAIR COLOR?

SMURFETTE HAS BREAKFAST WITH PAPA SMURF!

I sold out!

What would the press smurf without Smurfette?

THE SMURF PRESS

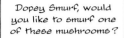

Panel 1: Dopey Smurf, would you like to smurf one of these mushrooms?

Panel 2: :Crunch...:

Panel 3: You don't feel a little sick?

No!

Panel 4: So, they're edible then!

© Peyo - 2000 Lic. IMPS (Brussels)

396

Panel 1: EUSMURFA! I've just discovered how to smurf electricity!

Panel 2: Awesome! What a coincidence!

?

Panel 3: That's just what I was needing!

© Peyo - 2001 Lic. IMPS (Brussels)

487

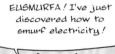

89

Panel 1: An umbrella?! Come on, Dopey Smurf, it's broad daylight!

:PFF!: He's so dumb!

Panel 2: Yes, but it's the Fall!

© Peyo 1998 - Lic. IMPS (Brussels)

I'm going to smurf you some advice about mushrooms!

BLAM

First suggestion: never sit on a puffball mushroom!

© Peyo - 1998 Lic. IMPS (Brussels)

229

Thanks to this book, you can smurf your odd jobs by yourself! Call me if you need help.

DO IT YOUR-SELF

Handy Smurf, I need help!

© Peyo - 2001 Lic. IMPS (Brussels)

A25

Me, I don't like this stupid game!

Do you hear me, Lazy Smurf?

Z Z Z

© Peyo - 2002 Lic. IMPS (Brussels)

554

I have two alarms in case I break one.

Two keys in case I lose one.

Two wheelbarrows in case I wear one out.

579

© Peyo

633

DANGER FALLING ROCKS!

© Peyo - 2003 Lic. IMPS (Brussels)

663

© Peyo

Lazy Smurf! Sleeping again?! Do you want me to smurf you what this book says about sleeping?

"Sleep is a necessary activity that resmurfs the organism's strength, and…"

Z

© Peyo - 2003 Lic. IMPS (Brussels)

600

Papa Smurf! Greedy Smurf is walking in his sleep.

He's a sleepwalker. We mustn't wake him!

ZZZ Z...

ZZZ Z...

He's eating cakes in his sleep!

I'm starting to have my doubts!

YUM CHOMP glp CRUNCH YUM

© Peyo - 1998 Lic. IMPS (Brussels)

There! That's all for today.

But you only worked for five minutes!

You can't work on a sunrise for more than five minutes a day!

SNAP

© Peyo - 2001 Lic. IMPS (Brussels)

Hey, Hefty Smurf, you don't know a way to smurf hiccups?

?

Sorry, that's the only way I know!

But?...

Maybe, but I'm not the one with hiccups! It's Greedy Smurf!

© Peyo - 2001 Lic. IMPS (Brussels)

Strip 234:

Papa Smurf, Papa Smurf! The ball! Smurf me a pass!

?

© Peyo - 1998 Lic. IMPS (Brussels)

234

Strip 353:

Oh! A birdcall!

I wonder what animal it can smurf?

Yes? What is it? What's going on?

© Peyo - 2000 Lic. IMPS (Brussels)

353

Strip 126:

Greedy Smurf, Papa Smurf has already told you that you shouldn't eat too much. Otherwise, you'll get big and fat, you'll be sick, and you'll come down with gout!

I'll tell him you're not listening to what he says.

YUM! GULP

CRUNCH

And I'll also tell him that you don't listen to what I smurf to you either.

BURP

And most of all, I'll tell him you refused to smurf me a piece of cake!

© Peyo 1998 - Lic. IMPS (Brussels)

126

So, Sculptor Smurf, you see, you're not the only one who can smurf with a chisel!

Mmm... Yeah, not bad! But the nose is a little big.

A little tap with the chisel, and it'll be quickly fixed!

Hey! No! It was a joke!

Darn it!

x

Say, would you please smurf this envelope to Papa Smurf's house?

Of course!

You're sweet! And here, that's for the stamp...

Smurfette, wait... there's an extra charge because of the size!

Handy Smurf, have you fixed my glasses?

Uh... No, not yet!

Well, get a smurf on. It's urgent!

Fine, fine, okay!

670

I'm fed up with reading like this! What's more, the fish smurfs in front of the text all the time!

© Peyo - 2003 Lic. IMPS (Brussels)

?

?

?

© Peyo - 1998 Lic. IMPS (Brussels)

21

I'd like to smurf a present for Smurfette! Can you help me?

For me?

Yes! It's an anti-wrinkle cream!

Uh... I also have a salve for black eyes, if you want...

?

© Peyo - 2003 Lic. IMPS (Brussels)

593

This makes me happy, Lazy Smurf! You're the only Smurf who wants to listen to my music! So, a waltz? A toccata? Some Bela Bartok?

A lullaby!

163

RAM BLAM PATPLAM! RAM PLAM! ANNOUNCEMENT FOR ALL SMURFS!

What's the smurf?

I don't know, but it sounds serious...

RAM PLAM PLAM! Announcement for all Smurfs! Whoever smurfed my drumsticks is asked to bring them back!

Go ahead, Clumsy Smurf! The most important thing with the hammer throw is the speed of rotation.

!

26

One little detail: you must let go of the hammer!

© Peyo - 1998 Lic. IMPS (Brussels)

What's going on, Smurfette?

Come now, say something! What's got you all smurfed up like this?

Hmm... I see. You mistook the glue stick for your lipstick!

677

© Peyo - 2003 Lic. IMPS (Brussels)

Papa Smurf says to pick only the red berries and to leave the black ones.

Bah! What's the difference?

He said the black berries aren't edible.

!

And... Papa Smurf... is always... right... and--

Shut up and run!

© Peyo - 2001 Lic. IMPS (Brussels)

415

?

Ha ha! A fake hole! Good try, Jokey Smurf, but it didn't work!

© Peyo - 1998 Lic. IMPS (Brussels)

232

Lazy Smurf! Smurfing again? It's shameful. You're nothing but a smurf-potato! You should follow my example and do some exercise.

I'll go right now!

© Peyo - 1998 Lic. IMPS (Brussels)

© Peyo

⸘SNIRRFFF!⸻

© Peyo - 2003 Lic. IMPS (Brussels)

Hey, you! So, you don't have a handkerchief?!

Of courf I 'ave a 'ankerchief! ⸘Sniff!⸻

Oh! Well then?

Well den what? If you fink I'm gonna loan it to you...

151

And a bird in the hand is worth two in the smurf, and what's more, smurf me once, shame on you, smurf me twice...

Because, as Papa Smurf always says... **?**

HA HA! Okay, you got me, Jokey Smurf!

How the heck did he recognize me?

359

CRUNCH YUM! YUM! CHOMP

You're smurfing your time, Hefty Smurf! Smurfette doesn't want to go out with anybody tonight.

Let me smurf! You'll see, I'm going to charm her by smurfing her a serenade.

Okay! Okay, I accept, Harmony Smurf! But for mercy's sake, no more serenade!

That's not fair! She's smurfing under duress!

My smurfness, Greedy Smurf! We're only leaving for a day!

A whole day? And he's just telling me now? I didn't smurf enough supplies to last that long!

Well, then? Heh heh! What do you smurf of that?

Not bad, but you could have taught him to applaud at the end of his number like real sea lions!

A gift for me? That's smurfly kind, Jokey Smurf!

:Pfff...: Hee hee hee!

A necklace? But I don't understand?

?! For smurf's sake, I mistook the gift!

Brainy Smurf, you haven't seen Jokey Smurf?!

?

© Peyo - 2002 Lic. IMPS (Brussels)

482

There are still a few lovely cherries right at the tip of the tree!

Yes, that's right!

We ought to be able to smurf up there with the tallest ladder!

Yes, no doubt!

© Peyo - 2003 Lic. IMPS (Brussels)

I think we'll leave them for the birds!

Yes, that would be better!

667

?

THE SMURFS AND ROBOT X-XIII

Hey! Look, Lazy Smurf, it's the saucer of your buddy, BRTT, the ET! It looks like he's having a problem. He's going to smurf into the pond!

Hmm! Huh... What?

BROP

BROB Bzz Bzz

BROOP

PL'OOF

Oh, he's not alone! Smurf me your hand, BRTT!

TH..NK Y..., FR...NDS!

!

Oh! What's that flying smurf?

H.D., H.D.! TH.Y.R. L..K.NG F.R .S!

BRTT says he ran away from his planet with Bizouline, his fiancée, because Prince Azor, Bizouline's father, doesn't smurf of their marriage! He smurfed his spaceship to pursue them!

BZZ !

Oh! Look!

What's that smurf, BRTT?

X-XIII = B.D R.B.T!

BZZZZZZ

Peep

VWeeet

See "The Smurf from Outer Space" on page 99

See "The Smurf from Outer Space" on page 99

TCHAF

BZZZZZ

TWEET TWEET

© Peyo

1

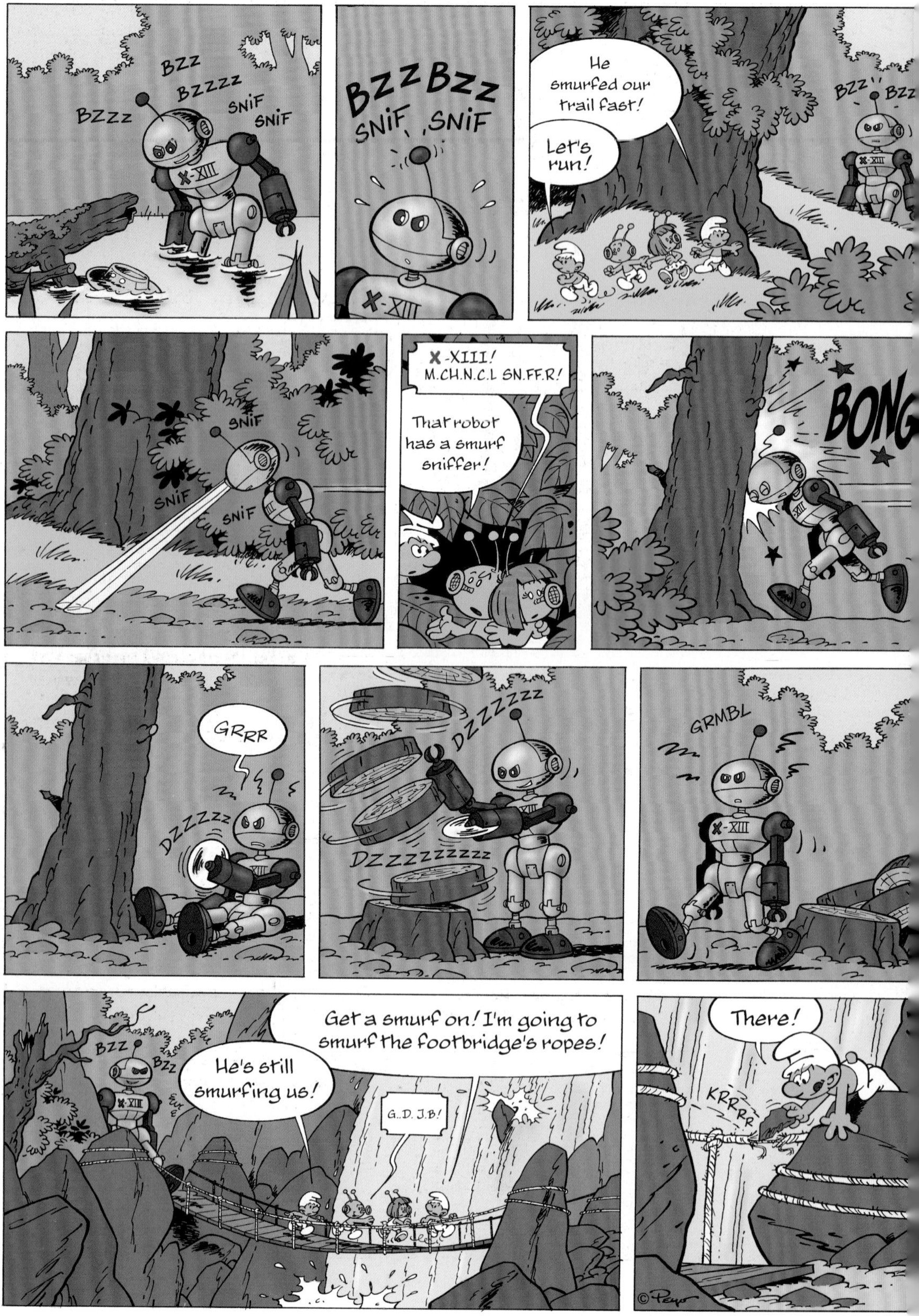
BZZ
BZzzz
BZzz
SNiF
SNiF
BZZBZZ
SNiF ,SNiF
X-XIII
He smurfed our trail fast!
Let's run!
BZZ BZZ
X-XIII
SNiF
SNiF
SNiF
X-XIII!
M.CH.N.C.L SN.FF.R!
That robot has a smurf sniffer!
BONG
GRRR
DZZZZZZ
DZZZZZ
DZZZZZZZZZ
GRMBL
X-XIII
BZZ
BZZ
X-XIII
Get a smurf on! I'm going to smurf the footbridge's ropes!
He's still smurfing us!
G..D. J.B!
There!
KRRRR
© Peyo

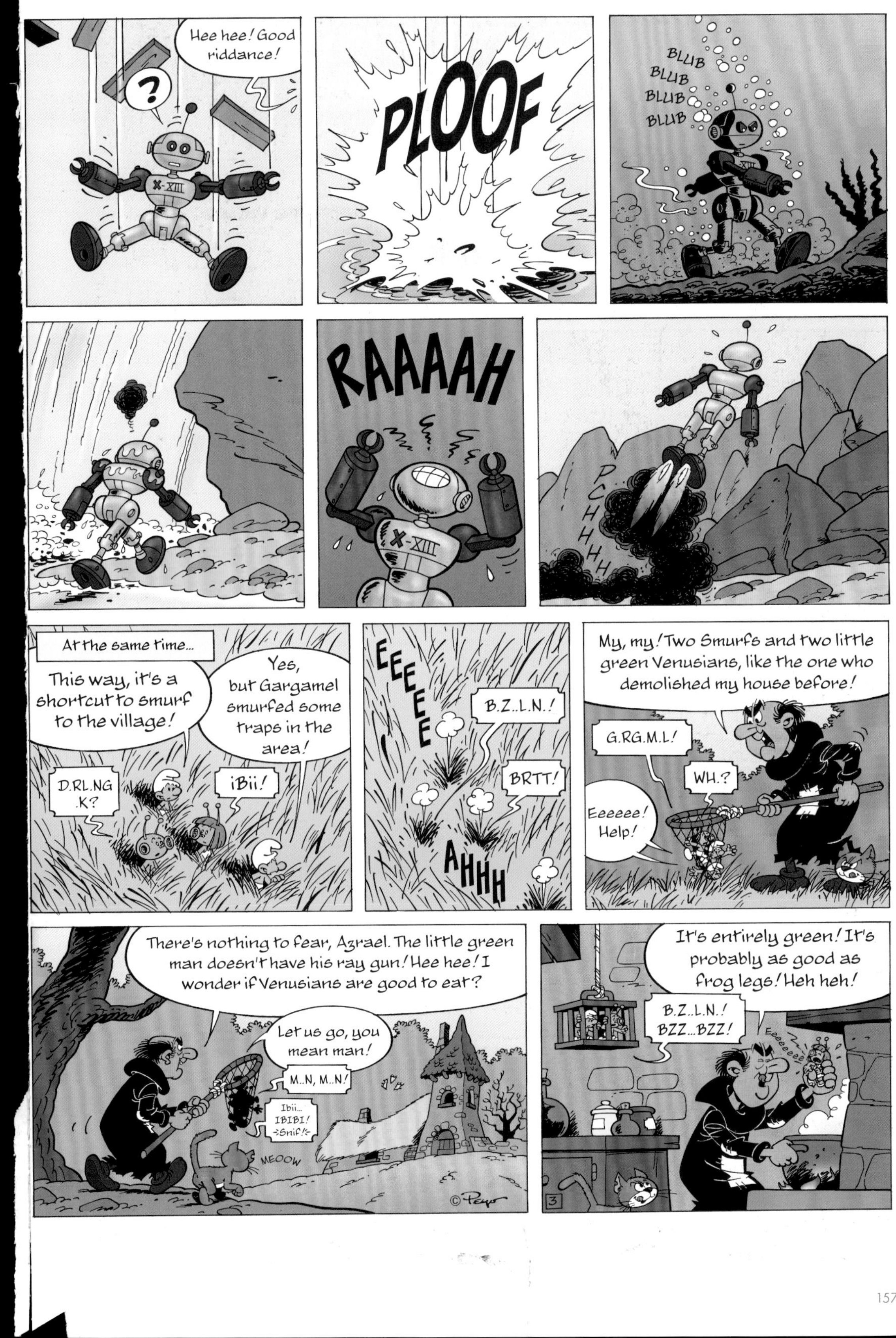

?
Hee hee! Good riddance!
PLOOF
BLUB BLUB BLUB BLUB
RAAAAH
PCHHHHH
At the same time...
This way, it's a shortcut to smurf to the village!
Yes, but Gargamel smurfed some traps in the area!
D.RL.NG .K?
¡Bii!
EEEEEE
B.Z..L.N.!
BRTT!
AHHH
My, my! Two Smurfs and two little green Venusians, like the one who demolished my house before!
G.RG.M.L!
WH..?
Eeeeee! Help!
There's nothing to fear, Azrael. The little green man doesn't have his ray gun! Hee hee! I wonder if Venusians are good to eat?
Let us go, you mean man!
M..N, M..N!
Ibii... IBIBI! Snif!
MEOOW
© Peyo
3
It's entirely green! It's probably as good as frog legs! Heh heh!
B.Z..L.N.! BZZ...BZZ!

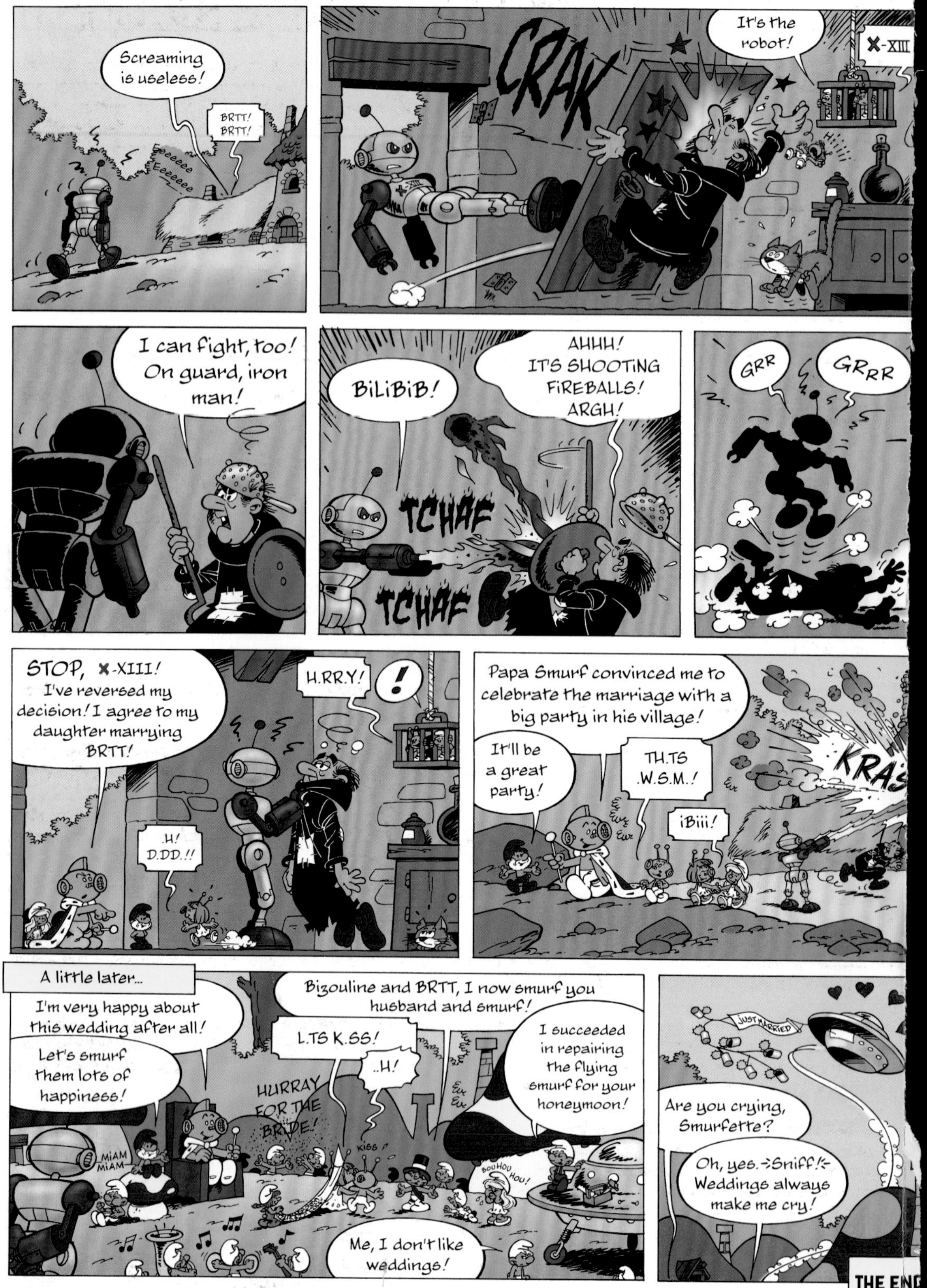

Screaming is useless!
BRTT! BRTT!
Eeeeee Eeeeee Eeeeee
CRAK
It's the robot!
X-XIII
I can fight, too! On guard, iron man!
BiLiBiB!
AHHH! IT'S SHOOTING FIREBALLS! ARGH!
TCHAF
TCHAF
GRR
GRRR
STOP, X-XIII! I've reversed my decision! I agree to my daughter marrying BRTT!
H.RR.Y!
!
.H! D.DD.!!
Papa Smurf convinced me to celebrate the marriage with a big party in his village!
It'll be a great party!
TH.TS .W.S.M.!
iBiii!
A little later...
I'm very happy about this wedding after all!
Let's smurf them lots of happiness!
Bizouline and BRTT, I now smurf you husband and smurf!
L.TS K.SS!
..H!
HURRAY FOR THE BRIDE!
I succeeded in repairing the flying smurf for your honeymoon!
MIAM MIAM
KISS
BOUHOU HOU!
Me, I don't like weddings!
JUST MARRIED
Are you crying, Smurfette?
Oh, yes. -Sniff!- Weddings always make me cry!
THE END
4

WATCH OUT FOR PAPERCUTZ™

Welcome to the sixth smurftastic volume of THE SMURFS TALES by Peyo—the graphic novel series featuring the original Smurfs comics that inspired the new hit Nickelodeon TV series (plus other Peyo creations such as *Johan and Peewit* and *Benny Breakiron*), now in its second successful season. THE SMURFS TALES is brought to you by Papercutz, the smurfy folks dedicated to publishing great graphic novels for all ages. I'm Jim Salicrup. The Smurf-in-Chief, here to reflect a bit on how creating comics has changed, from when first Peyo started producing comics to today, when Peyo's studio continues in his Smurftastic tradition...

Way back in the pre-digital days when I used to edit comics, lots of things were different, and lots of things were the same. Obviously, one of the biggest differences was that everything was done on paper, not computers, back then. (Gee, maybe we should call ourselves Digicutz?)

Writers typed their scripts on paper, then mailed them to their editor. The editor would edit the script, usually with a blue pencil, then mail the edited script to the artists.

The artists would pencil the comics on art boards (paper such as Strathmore) then mail the pages to the editor.

The editor would send the script with the penciled pages to the letterer, who would letter the pages in ink, then send back to the editor.

The editor would send the lettered pages to an inker, who would embellish the pencils with black ink, so that they can better be reproduced, then send back to the editor.

The editor then would send copies of the black and white inked pages to the colorist, who would provide color guides for the color separators.

The editor would proofread the lettered pages, and after any corrections were made, usually by an in-house production department, the artwork and color guides were then sent to the color separators and then on to the printer.

That was then, this is now:

Writers typed their scripts on their computer, then emailed them to their editor. The editor would edit the script, usually on their computer, then email the edited script to the artists.

The artists would either pencil the comics on art boards (paper such as Strathmore) and then scan the art and email the pages to the editor or use a computer, such as a Wacom tablet to create the art digitally then email the pages to the editor.

The editor would email the script with the art pages to the letterer and the colorist at the same time, the letterer would letter the pages on their computer, then send back to the editor, while the colorist colors the pages usually in a program such as PhotoShop, and then emails the pages back to the editor.

The colored and lettered pages would then be merged by a production person, and then sent to the editor.

The editor would proofread the lettered pages and colored pages, and after any corrections were made, usually by the letterer and colorist, the completed artwork files would be sent digitally via WeTransfer or posted online where the printer can digitally access the files (places such as ShareFile).

And unlike before, when once the interior pages were sent to the printer, the next time the editor saw the work again, it was already printed. Now, the editor gets to see a digital proof, mainly to catch any last mistakes, but mostly to be sure the pages are all in the right order, no repeated pages, no missing pages, to make sure the double page spreads actually face each other, etc. and everything is ready to be printed.

But the one thing that hasn't changed is the comics themselves. We still strive to create the best stories possible, by working with the very best writers, artists, colorists, letterers around the world! Just check out the next volume of THE SMURF TALES to see for yourself!

Smurf you later,

Jim

STAY IN TOUCH!

EMAIL: salicrup@papercutz.com
WEB: papercutz.com
TWITTER: @papercutzgn
INSTAGRAM: @papercutzgn
FACEBOOK: PAPERCUTZGRAPHICNOVELS

Go to papercutz.com and sign up for the free Papercutz e-newsletter!

THE SMURFS GRAPHIC NOVELS AVAILABLE FROM PAPERCUTZ™

THE SMURFS 3 IN 1 VOL. 1

THE SMURFS 3 IN 1 VOL. 2

THE SMURFS 3 IN 1 VOL. 3

THE SMURFS 3 IN 1 VOL. 4

THE SMURFS 3 IN 1 VOL. 5

THE SMURFS 3 IN 1 VOL. 6

THE SMURFS 3 IN 1 VOL. 7

THE SMURFS TALES #1

THE SMURFS TALES #2

THE SMURFS TALES #3

THE SMURFS TALES #4

THE SMURFS TALES #5

THE SMURFS TALES #6

THE SMURFS TALES #7

THE SMURFS 3 IN 1 graphic novels are available in paperback only for $14.99 US each at booksellers everywhere. THE SMURFS TALES graphic novels are avaialble in paperback for $14.99 each and $22.99 each for hardcover at booksellers everywhere. Or order from us. Please add $5.00 for postage and handling for the first book, add $1.00 for each additional book. Please make check payable to NBM Publishing. Send to: PAPERCUTZ, 160 Broadway, Suite 700, East Wing, New York, NY 10038 (1-800-886-1223).

THE SMURFS graphic novels are also available digitally from COMIXOLOGY.com as well as at ebook sellers everywhere.

WWW.PAPERCUTZ.COM